MW01248170

The Brewers' Murder Diaries

The Brewers' Murder Diaries

David Slocum

Sun Brewing Company

Contents

Contents

Chapter 1.

The Brewers' Murder Diaries.
Dear Diary,
The murder began over a sour ale at the Sun Brewing Motel.
She was an attractive lady. It's too bad she had bad taste buds.
The neon motel sign shone brightly over the shadowy rustic Sun Brewing Pub and Motel. The establishment was tucked away from town in the borderlands, right on the railroad tracks on the Rio Grande in Canutillo, Texas. The crossroads to Mexico, Texas, and New Mexico.

She walked up in bright red heels, so freakin' high she could barely walk without fumbling. She was one of those cheugy millennials, still youngish but not quite pulling off her body-tight green dress with garish cutouts that strained against her healthy curves. If not being trendy is a bad thing, then I guess I liked bad things.

I was sitting on the front patio enjoying a porter. I slowly grinned because the desert sky was putting on a beautiful light show for us with its fading blues and its red clouds. It was the perfect setting for putting on the Sun Brewing charm. Peter François Amador, the motel manager, was already outside talking to some other guests, and he came over to greet the newcomer. Everyone loves Peter. He's a little person with a killer wit, and he's extremely charismatic. Peter is truly a renaissance man. He is an artist with his finger paintings, he has a master's degree, and he was a top-notch gymnast in college. Peter has impeccable style and taste to go with his perfect old-world table manners (which are a key part of his charm for guests). If he had a weakness it would be that he has little to no tolerance for rudeness.

Peter with his Goldilocks hair and soft eyes welcomes the woman in red heels with her long silky black hair and that green dress. Peter books Isabella Mata a room and shows her the beer on tap and the motel's finest bottles of ale and lager in the fridge.

Isabella said slowly, OMG do you have a bottle opener? Peter replied, You have a lovely accent; it's almost like a real Spaniard. If you prefer Spanish, I can entertain you with mine—or some other language, if you like? I speak several languages fluently. Let me show you the bottle opener for these spontaneous ales. To no surprise she is a fresa. Isabella Mata from Mexico City is a classic fresa and is dressed to die for. A real attention grabber. A short tight green dress cut short to show off her legs and shape.

Peter checks her in, then gives her a motel tour, including the brewery. Isabella doesn't seem impressed with too much but Rupprecht Von Wallenrodt, one of the assistant brewers, tries real hard to impress her with his knowledge. Rupprecht also is an expert at beer sensory; he can taste and evaluate beers for any flaws. He poured a Wiener lager from the fermenter into a small tasting goblet, then started explaining the beer and offered her a taste. She ignores him. Rupprecht is an Afro-German and Bavarian trained brewer. His parents are German immigrants, and he comes from a long line of brewers. Rupprecht's family lives in the borderlands. Rupprecht is without question a huge asset when it comes to traditional European brewing. Rupprecht loves to explain history and is now explaining to Isabella how Mazatlán is truly a German settlement from the early 16th century, with Spaniards and indigenous people. Soon he is describing how the Mexican lager is really a long lost Vienna lager originating from Austria in the 1830s, which is around the forming of the new country of Mexico.

Rupprecht treats everyone like they are all in a game show called Beer Jeopardy. Eventually, he notices the thousand-yard stare on Isabella's face and starts apologizing to her. But here comes Jon Miguel Baio, who doesn't care about social cues and is looking at Isabella like a kid who sees a lollipop. He gives me the vibes of a future stalker. He's a former Navy Seal drifter who connected well with the owner, Billy Bob Dankworth, and Billy Bob gave him a shot as Rupprecht's brewer's assistant. Jon has little filter but means well.

When Rupprecht stops talking, Jon jumps in and tells her how much he loves her hair and how it goes well with her dress. She says she borrowed it from a friend. He says, Nice! And then, Do you think you could help me with the volume of my hair? And then, Hey, I got melons! You like melons?

She finally broke a smile and Jon explained he was having watermelon for a snack if she would like to partake in a beer and melon. She said maybe, I'll be around, and Peter advised her to watch out for his dark proclivities then escorted her away. Rupprecht put his arm around Jon and said, Let me give you some advice, kid: No matter how many giggles you get for chugging beers, try not to slurp so loud or belch in anyone's face. And clean the watermelon from your mug as you eat. That's a lot of woman for you. Jon replied, Some women don't like guys like me, but Rupp, some girls do!

Peter and Isabella enter the restaurant and bar area where he introduces her to Chino. Ruben "Chino" Aragon is the head bartender and a beloved local personality. Chino was made to be a bartender, he is street smart, loyal, funny, personable, and a very close friend of Billy Bob. Chino is also a former inmate, one of those dudes who went down the wrong path at a young age as a troubled youth but truly isn't a bad person. Billy Bob and Chino go way back and are both bikers. Chino rides his Harley every single day of his life, while Billy Bob usually drives his green 1970 Volkswagen Beetle to work.

Peter introduces Isabella to Chino, and she says, Are you really Chinese? Do people around here ever tell you to go back to China? Chino laughs and says, Sure, ever once in a while, somebody visiting like you will ask for a bloody lip. I live on that dirt road over there by the Rio Grande in a cute little ranch. You know what I call it? She says, What? And he smiles as he looks around at the room, everyone of whom is in on the joke, and says, Back to China. I go Back to China every night, ma'am. Less'n it's a good night.

He enjoyed his laugh and she smiled indulgently. He said, I was born and raised here in the Borderlands. Did you know there are a lot of Asian immigrants in Mexico? They helped a lot with construction especially the Chinese with the Railroads. Isabella doesn't respond and only listens. They've also contributed greatly to the Mexican cuisine, ever hear of chamoy sauce? ..and why do you think chiles toreados has soy sauce? Isabella just smiles.

Where are you from Isabella? You sound like you're from Spain. He leans over and whispers to Peter, She is a fresa, huh?

Isabella said, I'm from Mexico City.

Chino, with a huge smile, said, I've always wanted to go there, especially to see the Aztec pyramids. What brings you to the Sun Brewing Motel, Isabella?

I'm traveling to Denver to visit my cousins but wanted to be a tourist here in the borderlands.

What made you choose the Sun Brewing Motel as a tourist?

I've read a lot about this place, actually. It has a mystique to it, but I'm not accustomed to these types of places.

Chino replies, Why is that?

IIt's like being in a dive bar... just look at all the people in here. It's like a zoo designed by an old cowboy!

Chino laughs again and says, Yes it is! Giraffes, lambs, cuckoo birds, and lions all in the same dive. Chino takes a slight bow and nods at her, ending their conversation.

Billy Bob rides up on his chopper blasting Iron Maiden's "Writing on the Wall" as Isabella walks to the patio and is greeted by Maggie Sanchez, the waitress. Maggie waves at Billy Bob, saying, Thank goodness, Billy Bob is back. Isabella talks to Maggie in Spanish and Maggie politely tries to reciprocate in her broken Spanglish. Isabella laughs and tells Maggie to forget it, English is fine. What do you recommend Maggie? Well, says Maggie, Billy Bob, the owner and head brewer, is an international award-winning brewer known for his sour ales. How about Le Figaro, a prickly pear sour ale? Prickly pears are grown here locally; Billy Bob loves to use the ingredients from the borderlands. Sounds exotic, says Isabella. Sure, I'll give it a try.

Maggie puts in the order and Billy Bob himself brings it out in a stemmed glass, waving his free hand and singing, Figaro, Feee-garo... Feeegaro... La la la la la la la! Maggie brings some house tostada chips and salsa and sets it on the table as Isabella takes a sip of the sour ale—and spits it out!

It splattered everywhere, including on Billy Bob's shirt and Maggie's pants. OMG, says Isabella, I was expecting something more like lemonade! Maggie apologizes and tells her she won't be charged for the beer and that she'll find a beer that will be more acceptable to her. Maggie brings her a table lager, explaining, This is our motel table lager; it's very sessionable. Isabella still seems irked, perhaps because she isn't sure what *sessionable* means, but at least she is pacified for now. She orders Chef Billy Bob's Tacos du Jour.

Billy Bob again personally exits the kitchen and brings over a plate of tacos. For the lovely lady, he says, I present my signature goat-head tacos. She's in disbelief. Billy Bob says, Just think of it like tacos de machitos in Mexico. Isabella notices Billy Bob eyes and is once again astonished. I never seen a person with different colored eyes before, she says. You have one hazel-brown eye and one blue eye. Billy Bob responds, So I've been told. Actually, it's called heterochromia; I was born this way. Isabella turns to the goat-head tacos but is not having anything to do with them. She points a finger to her wide-open mouth and tells Billy Bob, I'll order pizza from somewhere else. Your salsa wasn't even that good.

Billy Bob was infuriated and began to lecture her. Listen, now that is my traditional Mexican salsa, made with roasted tomatoes, onions, garlic, and jalapeños in a molcajete with lime juice and cilantro! It was my grandma's recipe!

Where's your abuela now?

She's dead!

Choked on the salsa, did she?

Billy Bob is kind of a unique guy. He's half hillbilly from the Deep South, Alabama, and Tennessee, while his mother is Chicana from El Paso. He's bilingual and always talking about how he grew up on fried chicken and tamales—but he could be very sensitive. I can see him now... the way he was always complaining how hillbillies are a marginalized people. Any time he is insulted he assumes it's because people think he's a dumb hillbilly, then he walks away muttering to himself because he is incapable of controlling his tongue—or his fists—when he gets really pissed.

He grabs Isabella's plate of tacos and walks away muttering to himself. It's really comical to see. He never uses curse words; it's always some kind of silly substitute like *corksucker, further murking, gull darn communist.* He calls his new guest a *sucking witch.*

Sundays are for oldies. Billy Bob loves oldies, especially listening to Mike G on the jukebox on a Sunday afternoon, but he's strange in that he is someone who can listen to oldies then flip to heavy metal. Billy Bob goes back to his kitchen with the tacos du jour and changes the patio music from Elvis's "Don't be Cruel" to Hatebreed's "In Ashes They Shall Reap." That's a clue Billy Bob is pissed and hurt and going to go home to his lovely wife and kids and cry about how somebody didn't like his food and beer. Billy Bob is someone who doesn't take people not liking his food—and especially his beer—lightly. He's a family man and a great philanthropist; Billy Bob always gives free meals to the homeless. Anybody down on their luck and needs a hot plate, he will give them one with no questions asked. But he cannot handle criticism of his beer and cuisine. We'll all never hear the end of it if someone doesn't like his creations. He'll walk off muttering, then he'll start talking to himself for the rest of the day. That's Billy Bob, for better or worse.

Isabella goes back to her room but comes back to the bar later in the evening. She turns a lot of heads, drinks some more table lager, and listens to Ray Monroe's solo classic acoustic guitar act. Ray went to high school with Billy Bob and is a local musician. Isabella teases him and asks him to play Kanye West's "Heartless," but Ray just smiles and starts in on his own rock 'n' roll version.

Jon Miguel finally makes it to the patio to drink some beers with Isabella, but she has just received a phone call from her ex-boyfriend, which for some reason she takes. She talked quite a bit with him, but finally she ended the call, saying, I seriously have to go now, I'm hanging out with my new friend Jon. If I were Jon I'd be hoping the ex doesn't know where to find him about now.

Isabella finally starts to warm up and be approachable. Jon asked, How old are you, Isabella? You look 21. Isabella smiled and said, I'm 27. No, I'll go ahead and break the suspense: I'm 31. What do you do for a living, Isabella? I'm in college studying forensic science. Oh, wow! That's interesting, what are you learning? I've learned I have Mexican cheek bones. Let me understand you correctly: The Spaniards sail across the Atlantic to form a man-made concept of a country but your cheek bones survived colonization for 200 years? Isabella replied, That's correct. This new learning amazes me, Señorita Isabella! I think the Navy affected my DNA; I should look into that forensic stuff. My great great grandpappy was in the Navy and we all have sailor's forearms.

Very impressive.

I used to be a Navy Seal. Now I'm a brewer, can you believe that? Billy Bob walks by on his way to see his wife and says, Meeeguel, try to get some rest tonight. We have a brew day tomorrow. Jon tells Isabella, I don't know why he keeps calling me *Meeguel*. Isabella smiles. Isabella for the first time is actually likeable; she is smiling and tolerant. Jon is making small talk and asking Isabella if she would ever consider sky diving with him after he drinks a six pack. Isabella replies, You're charming Jon. I like you. Well, Isabella, I drink, and I know how to jump out of planes. You ready to ravage the town, Isabella?

Jon, what's the deal with this place? Everything in the motel seems to be from the 70s. There's a rotary phone and a cuckoo clock in my room. That's all Billy Bob, he loves the 70s for some reason. Okay, Isabella, time to prowl.

No, thank you. I'd rather just walk on the railroad tracks and hang out on the river. It's a beautiful night. I've never seen railroad tracks so close to a river and so close to a motel at the same time before. You're right, Isabella. There's a moon out tonight; let's go throw rocks in the river and drink some more beer.

Jon grabbed a tall-can four-pack of lager and they walked down toward the river.

I've heard you've had a rough day today, he said. Yeah, your Billy Bob is an intense person, and I think he hates me. Well, I don't hate you Isabella. Billy Bob just needs to talk to himself for a few minutes or call his wife. I don't know how Billy Bob is functional, he always has a beer in his hand and is often times obtuse. I've seen him piss himself passed out in a bush off the side of the road. Stuff happens, I guess but I hope you're enjoying your stay. Isabella stops. I'm getting tipsy, I should probably get back to my room. What! The night has just begun. I'm not going to turn into a were-wolf, although there is a full moon out tonight. Isabella replies, I'm tired but thank you for your company, Jon.

She eventually stumbles her way back to her room for the night. The next morning when it's time for checkout, Bianca Casas, the cleaning lady, knocks on the door because it's past checkout and she needs to clean the room. Bianca notices Isabella's belongings are still in the room. The bed smells like urine with the sheets messed up and a gag ball in the middle of the bed. Bianca's Tourette's kicks in as she yells, Holy dodo dingbat kaka balls lick apples pissfarts! There were many such fragments spoken loud and fast, which is not uncommon for Bianca when she gets excited. Everyone knows about Bianca's condition, but everyone loves her. She is a super hard worker and always doing for others. She means well and is extremely well liked. She's always helping others.

Bianca skips the room cleaning and reports it to Peter.

When they come back to the room, Isabella hasn't returned. Peter notices a note in the center of the bed that is of burned antique paper and written in calligraphy that reads;

There is nothing more intimate than from my hands to yours.

Like songbirds singing in the cornfields, it's pure euphoria and attraction.

A chemical romance and chain reaction.

...the note along with her wallet and personal items are still in the room. Peter reports it to Billy Bob. Days pass, and at last they call the police to file a missing person's report. Days turn into weeks and still no Isabella.

Jose "Pepe" Martinez III and his son Jose "Pepe" Martinez IV ride up on their horses Pepe III is the local police detective and his son, Pepe IV, is the deputy. Both sport bushy mustaches, but Pepe IV's is more like a Hungarian handlebar mustache, something a real hipster cowboy would sport. Detective Pepe is a real-life inspector Clouseau in most ways except his eating habits. Pepe III loves to eat a lot of donuts daily. He's a bit large, short, and un-athletic, and it's hard to imagine him literally chasing down a criminal. Pepe IV is also short, but he's fit and muscular and reminds one of a rattlesnake.

Peter greets and welcomes the Pepes. Pepe III seems to be on his own program and ignores him, fumbling around with items in the foyer that have no obvious relevance to a missing woman case. Pepe III asks Peter if he has any coffee, and Peter says, Of course, would you also like a donut with your coffee? Both Pepes said yes at the same time, then Detective Pepe said he likes his milky. Milky coffee and donuts coming up, says Peter. You're in luck. Billy Bob made fresh donuts this morning.

Peter returns with coffee and donuts. He says, I suppose investigations are like donuts; there are always holes in them. Det.

Pepe replies, Ah, ah! Except for the cream-filled ones. Those are sweet and easy. Det. Pepe invites Peter to sit down and asks him some preliminary questions about the day Isabella appeared—and disappeared.

They eventually ask to see Isabella's room, which Peter has studiously left untouched despite Billy Bob's eagerness to get a new customer in there. Peter is perplexed as he watches the Pepes clearly contaminate everything by picking up and moving things, not to mention their frequent passing of wind.

They return to the bar, where Billy Bob joins them. They search the area and seem astonished by the three 10-foot tall concrete egg fermenters outside on the patio. Pepe asks, What's up with the dinosaur eggs? Billy Bob explains, They're used for my 100% spontaneous ale fermentations. He slaps the side of one and says, These exotic ales take years to mature. They're like a fine wine... they just get better with age. Pepe asks, But why an egg? I'm glad you asked! The shape is of ancient origins dating back thousands of years in the history of fermentation. It's believed the shape helps insulate and stabilize fermentations by continuous circulation for the long haul. The shape also allows for superior texture and complexity through convection. He points to the window on the porthole. It's amazing to watch the continuous convention-flow fermentation work its magic bubblies. It's truly divine.

Pepe IV said, I don't suppose you could fit a person in one of those? Well, said Billy Bob, you can kind of climb in through this bottom door to clean them. When was the last time they were filled? These? They've been full for months.

Peter was unnerved by this line of questioning, but Billy Bob seemed more amused. Pepe IV continued, You couldn't fit a person through that top door up there? What? No, not unless they were pretty small, small as a kid. Anyway, it'd ruin the beer!

We wouldn't want that, said Pepe IV. Pepe III said, Hey, Billy Bob, you're not from around here, are you? Billy Bob immediately grew agitated and said, What's that? Oh, I'm from here, *Pee-Pee*, and I have my roots here, too. Pepe asked, That's *Pepe. Detective Pepe.* And I only ask because you have a slight southern accent. Okay, Pee-Pee, have it your way. I get my accent from my dad, who's Appalachian, but I was born here and grew up here. Pepe III muttered to Pepe IV, Hillbillies butcher the English language. Peter starts talking to Pepe and Billy Bob in Spanish, trying to calm things down. Pepe ignored Peter but told Billy Bob that he's going back to the room to take the gag ball in for evidence and that he'll be back for more clues. Billy Bob told Peter as Pepe was walking away that anyone named Pee-Pee has to be a pervert. Peter looked as if he had some thoughts about people named Billy Bob, too.

A month after the disappearance and the story has become a regional scandal, mostly because some web sleuths showed up at the motel and started snooping around with their amateur investigations and demanding justice in their YouTubes and TikToks. Some of them got interested in local Rio Grande ghost stories, the few we have. And they're starting to tell their own stories about the ghost of Isabella, who is officially still only missing.

Believe it or not, some of the podcasters mean business too. The Middles Open Podcast covers all things local in El Paso. TMO setup and did a live episode behind the Sun Brewing Motel dedicated to the disappearance of Isabella. Anthony Espalin, Peter and Abe Carrillo have hundreds of thousands of followers in the borderlands and when they do an episode people tune in. Luckily for Billy Bob and his motel, TMO takes an objective approach covering the story. The TMO guys with all their podcasts always inject an element of humor. That's why they also covered the ghost stories of the Rio Grande too as a plausible cause. Maybe they're giving Billy Bob the benefit of the doubt because he always sent TMO his beer and trying to convince them to do a "Breaking Beer News" segment in their podcast. Who knows, but Billy Bob doesn't feel they are out to get him.

Podcasters/web sleuths . They've all interviewed everyone from Sun Brewing and a number of local townsfolk and even the Pepes. Leading the charge is Ramona De la Hoya and her younger brother David. Ramona is short, petite and fiery. David is a little taller than Romana but a little chubby; he has Down's syndrome, which folks around here don't see much of, but he's won everyone over with his friendliness, which is in stark contrast to his sister's doggedness. Billy Bob told Ramona what he told everyone else: this place is a crossroads for many people. The Rio Grande at night is a dangerous place. He hoped nothing had happened to Isabella, but things do happen.

Real reporters from the papers and the TV news started showing up, too, asking their own questions. It was great for business, but eventually everyone at Sun Brewing grew tired of it all and pointed them to Detective Pepe for updates in the investigation.

Another brew day came around—we still have a business to run, after all. All Billy Bob ever wants to do is brew beer, and brew day is his labor of love day. His other favorite days are once a week, when they taste the beers in the secondary fermentation, and once a month, when they taste the spontaneous ales to see how they're progressing.

In addition to the three concrete egg fermenters outside, the Sun Brewing Motel also has three concrete cube-shaped fermenters, also part of their Spontaneous Ale Project. Rupprecht is taking his apprentice Jon to taste the spontaneous ale from the egg fermenters. Rupprecht explains to Jon that traditionally our 100% spontaneous ales have a little acetic and lactic acid sourness with a pinch of horse blanket funkiness from the brettanomyces wild yeast.

Rupprecht starts with the prickly pear sour ale. He pours straight out the fermenter into a goblet. He smells it and asks Jon to do the same. Jon doesn't know what to make of it other than it doesn't smell like anything he'd like to drink. Rupprecht explains to him the smell is way off even for a young spontaneous sour ale. Rupprecht tastes it and asks Jon to taste it as well. Rupprecht asks Jon what do you perceive? Jon regurgitates what he hears and says horse blanket. Rupprecht says no, that's butyric acid and tastes rancid. It tastes of moldy cheese, butter, and spoiled milk. This is a very bad beer. We are going to have to dump it, but first let's look inside so you can get a visual of symptoms of why this beer is so sinister.

They get the ladder and open the top of the fermenter and look inside.

There's something floating in there.

They've found Isabella.

Chapter 2.

Dear Diary,

I've always known there is something wrong with me, but I've also always known I have a conscience, although that doesn't change much. I find talking to my therapist not helpful in any meaningful way; it's uninteresting, boring. I've always had a strange feeling that every therapist I've ever talked to was deeply disturbed somehow. One therapy that works for me is talking to myself after ingesting a cold beer. Now that's very therapeutic!

Isabella, darling.

I asked Isabella a question: What do the letter E and a rubber ducky have in common?

She finally answered, You're a dummy.

Grandma always said, Iif you can't say something nice, then don't say anything at all. How close are you to your grandma?

Hmm...

It was somewhat of a difficult riddle, the answer I was looking for was: They both are in the middle of beer.

She didn't notice the tub filled with warm beer, a rubber ducky floating in the middle, before she had left her room. Yeah, people take beer baths at the Sun Brewing Motel. I was very disappointed because I wanted her to *observe the type of beer in the tub. It wasn't a deeply acidic ale—it was a special designed beer for fragrance and healing. People should know beer has all the essential nutrients for life and has healing powers. Literally, you can live off of beer.*

Even if she'd noticed the beer, I suspect she wouldn't appreciate the style, or how the bath would have cleaned her hair because of the addition of a concoction of apricots and how she would have come out clean with a fruity fragrance.

One of the most important questions I ask anyone is how close you are to your grandma. I was very close to my grandma.

Detective Pepe and Deputy Pepe show up at the motel again now that Isabella's body has been found. They take another look over the property, but if they didn't do it right the first time, I have little confidence they'll do any better this time. Can you believe these guys with their horses and cowboy hats?

News stations galore. The press is having a heyday with all this. As are the podcasters and the trolls and everyone in town.

Pepe III is even more serious now. He's interviewing everyone informally here but wants everyone to come down to the station for an official interview starting tomorrow. I can't wait to hear his brilliant line of questioning. I'm guessing he'll need some help at diagnosing this situation, maybe from a professional criminal psychologist. Now that would be something.

Next day, the Sun Brewing Motel runs on a skeleton crew so everyone who saw Isabella can go down to the station. They push through a crowd of reporters and gather in the front hall. Billy Bob goes first, walking into Detective Pepe's office with a box of fresh donuts that he made to share with everyone. He holds up the box and says, I know you like my donuts. I see you have a pot of coffee. Pepe says, Yep, and thanks for the donuts. May I grab a cup, Detective? Sure, go ahead. Then we'll get started. Billy Bob pours himself a styrofoam cup, sips, and says, Mmm... all the while smiling impishly at Detective Pepe.

Where were you the night of Isabella's disappearance? the detective asks. I went home early that day and only worked about 12 hours, so approximately 6 p.m.

What vehicle were you driving when you left to go home? My wife picked me up. I didn't drive because my Volkswagen Beetle is at New Chapter Garage getting fixed by Joe and Abe. These guys are my longtime friends and I trust them to do all my work.

Is? Well, *was*. It's fixed now.

Did you go straight home? Yes, I went straight home and crashed on the sofa.

Did you leave home again for any reason? No, I stayed home all night until the next day's work.

Did you notice anything unusual that day? The only thing unusual was she didn't like my tacos or salsa and even more shocking was she didn't like my beer.

Is this a joke to you? No, sir. I don't joke about cooking or beer.

I see. Well, your tacos are definitely Tex-Mex, if you ask me. I prefer my Abuelo's carnitas. I ordered your carnitas several times and they're okay.

Billy Bob is irked. Do you know what subtext is detective? No, why? I hope you choke on that donut! I make them freakin' carnitas with a whole hog of mixed pig parts boiled in pig fat with chili grease. Then I fry them up a bit to give them a hint of crispiness on the outside. You gull darn know I make great carnitas, Pepe! There is nothing substandard about Tex-Mex, it's a great cuisine. Get off your high horse! An El Pasoan like me has a palate for such things.

Pepe responds, You hillbillies butcher the English language. I can't understand a word you say sometimes, Bill Bob. He adds, I think you just agreed with me, so that's good.

Billy Bob responds, Well, get a bilingual person in here then. I'll speak Spanish!

Who else do you know spoke to Isabella that night at the motel? A bunch of us; we're a friendly staff. But Jon was having beers with her that night. She might have told him something.

Get out of here, Billy Bob, and get Jon over here pronto!

Jon was already waiting outside, so Billy Bob sent him in on his way out. Det. Pepe started in on him almost before he sat down.

Where were you the night of Isabella's disappearance, Jon? I had beers with her on the Sun Brewing Motel patio, then we went to the Rio Grande behind the motel and drank more beer and star gazed.

What happened next? She wanted to go back to her motel room and call it night.

Did you walk her back to her motel room? When was that? Yeah, it was early, still. Around 9 p.m.

What happened next? Nothin'. She went into her motel room and I went home.

Did that make you angry? Were you expecting something more from her? No, no, nothing like that. She was sexy and all, but I thought I had another couple nights to make a move.

Did you leave home again for any reason? No, I went home and knocked out until the next day.

Who do you live with? Nobody, I live alone.

Did you notice anything unusual that day? The only thing unusual was she found me interesting and was very into me, or so I thought. Oh, also she had a phone call with her ex-boyfriend.

Tell me about this phone call, Jon. It was a long phone call, and I was getting impatient. I almost walked off to go mingle for a little while until she finished because they were talking so long. The conversation seemed intense, and then Isabella cut him off and told the guy she was sitting having drinks with me, which I wish she hadn't a done, but there you go. Then she got off the phone and finally started warming up to me.

I can see how that's unusual, Jon. You have that horseshoe mustache and Village People look to you. You eat your meals like a 4-year-old! You slurp your soup and burp as if you're the most appreciative person in all of China. We all know it's not out of appreciation Jon—you have no manners and was raised in a barn. It's hard to imagine she would be into you, to be frank. That's probably why she called it a night early.

Jon bristled. You're wrong, Pepe. I was raised in a chicken shed! I was dirt poor, but I do have manners. Enough to know not to talk to folks like you do, Pepe.

Yeah, I'm a real roughneck. Now, who else do you know spoke to Isabella? Rupprecht was with her when I met her.

Very good. As possibly the last person who saw her, Jon, I'll be watching you! Don't leave town. I didn't do nothing to her, I promise. I certainly didn't stuff her in no fermenter. Do you know how long we'd been waitin' on that beer? It near broke Rupprecht's heart to dump it.

I'll send him flowers. Get out of here and send Rupprecht in.

Rupprecht came in looking truly aggrieved over the lost beer...or something.

Rupprecht, have a seat. When was the last time you seen Isabella? I saw her only once, when she was getting a brewery tour from Peter.

Did you speak to her at all? Yes, briefly. I tried to describe our brewing process and our beers. She wasn't so interested.

That's it? That's all you spoke about? Yes, sir.

So, you never seen her or spoke to her again? That's correct.

You're a very well-groomed, sophisticated type, Rupprecht. Why are you here? Tell me about yourself.

I'm an Afro-German immigrant. My parents are from Hamburg and immigrated here to Canutillo because of business opportunities.

What business opportunities are *here*, Rupprecht? My father Claudius started an automation business here and we all come from a long line of Bavarian trained brewers.

You're not a hamburgler, are you Rupprecht? Rupprecht grimaced as if he'd heard that one too many times. Very funny, Detective Martinez. To have wit and a keen sense of humor.

Thank you, Rupprecht. You may go. Get Peter in here, ASAP. Rupprecht rose and left the room. Peter soon entered.

Hello, Peter, have a seat. Thank you, Detective Martinez.

Did you notice anything strange at the motel while Isabella was there? Not at all, really, she was a pretty normal guest, maybe a little outspoken. But nothing unusual, no.

Did you like her? Like her? Were you attracted to her? Did it disappoint you that she had drinks with Jon that night? Oh, no, not really. I mean, she had her...charms, but she wasn't my type.

Of course she's not your type, you're a midget! How did you find out Isabella went missing? The cleaning lady Bianca Casas knocked on her door and nobody answered, so she went into the room and noticed all her personal belongings were still in the room. For example, her purse and luggage.

We found a ball gag in the room. Do you have any notion of where that came from? None at all, sir. People are into all sorts of things, I guess, but I don't know anyone personally into that kind of thing, and I certainly had no reason to imagine she was.

Why did Sra. Casas knock on her door? She cleans the rooms. It was past checkout, so she assumed it was empty, but we always knock before we enter a room that has recently been booked.

At what time did she knock on her door? At around noon, because noon is checkout.

Thank you, Peter. Please bring Señora Casas to me, ASAP.

Hola, Señora Casas, cómo está? Muy bien, gracias, Detective Martinez.

Did you notice anything unusual with Isabella or anything strange that night? Ay, Dios mío! Una cacahuata! No hay dos sin tres!

Oh, that's right, you have turrets.

Do you have anything to tell me that can be useful to help me solve this crime? The Rio Grande is filled with ghosts, Detective. El Cucuy is a curse in these lands, delivering vengeance along the Rio Grande. Some people believe El Cucuy lives in the rio and can see into your soul. If you've done wicked deeds, the Cucuy will come for you and take your soul.

You think El Cucuy took Isabella that night? Is El Cucuy into S&M, do you think? Please don't make fun, Detective. All I know is she pranced around the patio that night and the next morning I found her room a mess and her missing.

Nothing else? No, nada.

Gracias, Bianca. That's all. You can go.

Chapter 3.

Dear Diary,

It's taken a long time to get to this point. I'm going through a depression. I did seem happy, at least sometimes. For the most part, I enjoy certain people's conversation and I view myself as a people person—but others view me as an elitist being a snob to everyone. I'm not that at all, I just don't like many people—but I love talking to people...even though it's rare that happens.

It's the little things...that bother me.

Therapy doesn't help—therapy just allows me to pretend better. It's where I learn to respond to social cues and how to smile when I normally wouldn't consider it. It's a mystifying reality—I fool people, and people believe what they want to believe. Goes to show people fool themselves and only see what they want to see.

Medication helps, I guess, but has its highs and way too many lows.

The only real medication is beer and dancing with myself.

It's time to party like a beer drinking anti-superstar.

It's been weeks now, over a month since they found her body. The Pepes show up to the Sun Brewing Motel again and start snooping around, making their presence known. Peter runs to tell Billy Bob. Billy Bob told Rupprecht to take over. I'm going to make some stout beer donuts really quick, chocolate covered and sprinkled with nuts. See if that sweetens up our guest. I'll be back.

Detective Pepe finds Billy Bob in the kitchen and asks him, Hey, why do you have a hotdog stand on your patio if you have a kitchen? That's very observant, Pepe. On nice days, I work the hotdog stand and mini bar outside while the kitchen stays open for regular dishes. I make some gull darn good dogs in a snap. You have to come by for Frank N' Stein Fridays! I'm sure you've seen our mural of Frankenstein with a stein of beer in one hand and a Frankfurter in the other.

I have, yes. I didn't realize it was so literal. Detective Pepe, do you want a chocolate donut? I won't say no to a box—do you have coffee? Of course, it's up front by Chino. Billy Bob, I thought you might want to know that the finalized autopsy report will be ready next week. That's great! This has been bad press for my motel. Let's go get some coffee while we chat.

Billy Bob goes up front where Chino works. Dep. Pepe is sitting at the bar looking sullen. Billy Bob says, Hey, Chino. Chino is leaning against the bar enjoying a breakfast stout. Hey, Billy Bob, Detective! Beer Chugglers all the way, bro! Chino says, Hey, Detective Pepe, I think you forgot to interrogate me for the murder. I've been trying to convince your son, here, but he don't want to talk to me. Detective Pepe replied, Who said it was a murder? Chino responds, Aw, c'mon, detective. You don't think she got hot and decided to go swimming in our beer tank? Billy Bob chuckled, but then grew concerned and said, You're not, are you? Detective Pepe replies, No, of course not.

But you do offer beer baths, do you not? says Pepe, Jr. We do, yes, Billy Bob replies. You'll have to try it sometime. I suppose a beer swim isn't that different. No, I suppose not. Now what if someone found out Isabella was a little kinky and wanted to impress her. Mightn't it be romantic, and a little scandalous, to go skinny dipping in the beer vat, out under the stars? And suppose something goes wrong and she drowns. Well, you wouldn't want to be caught swimming in the beer *and* with a dead body, would you?

That is an elaborate theory, Deputy, says Billy Bob, but nobody here would be stupid enough to swim in a fermenter. There are active yeast cultures in there making sticky bubblies and more often than not pretty aggressive aromas. You ask me she was dumped in there after the fact by someone who wanted to make us look bad.

I know your theory, Billy Bob, says Detective Pepe, and I agree the odds are that Isabella was murdered and dumped in the tank later. It still seems likely it was done by someone she met here at The Sun Brewing Motel. Billy Bob, when can Chino come down to my office for an official statement? He can go now. Vamos, Chino!

Back at the station, Det. Pepe turns on his recorder. Chino, how do you know Billy Bob? We go way back, for decades. I've always had a rough time finding work because I'm a former inmate. I was working as a stalker at the Rio Grande supermarket, and I would always see Billy Bob coming into the store to buy groceries, but he always had a big backpack on. That's not something you see very often, so I would follow him around to see what he was up to. I would kind of lurk down the aisle from him, acting like I just happened to need something in the same aisles as him, but he caught on to me eventually. I followed him outside and seen him get on his Chopper, and I was like, Man, this guy is a biker like me! He started talking to me and we immediately became friends.

Why were you in prison, Chino? The judge called me a *menace to society*. When I was young, I was into selling drugs and had trash bags of weed for sale. I was also a person who didn't care if I lived or died. I got into fights, and I kept going to jail for violent crimes, but it wasn't because I was looking to hurt somebody, it was more like two guys that are not going to back down and someone was going to get hurt.

So, you're a violent criminal. No, not anymore. I was young and had a lot of problems. That's all behind me now.

Deputy Pepe jumped in. Billy Bob ever have a temper or get rough with folk? Billy Bob? No, man. I mean, he gets sore if you don't like his food, but he always walks away because he doesn't want to... Well, anyway, he's a stand-up guy. I remember him sponsoring a kick ball team, and we rounded up some of the guys and was going to convoy out to the game with his hotdog stand and beer. We loaded up the truck, then me, Mexican Mike, Chopper Bob, and Billy Bob put wigs on. We were going to ride through town to the game with wigs on. We got lost a bit because we were riding through El Paso central area, which as you know is a rough area.

So, we stop on this one block and get off our Harleys but we don't shut them off. These hard-core cholos are hanging out on the corner, and they tell us to shut off our lights! Billy Bob ignores them. They keep yelling at us, Shut off your lights! They start inching closer and closer, almost like sizing us up, but they couldn't see us clearly behind our headlights with the sun going down. They got close enough to where we started getting concerned. We're restaurant folk, not bangers, right? And I didn't want to get into no scrape and wind up back in jail, but I wasn't about to let no one tell me what to do with my Harley, either. They yelled again, For the last time turn off your lights!

Billy Bob said, If you come one step closer, I'm going to kill each and every one of you. Take one step closer, and you're dead. He said it like it was nothing, very serious but like he was doing them a favor giving them a warning. That stopped them in their tracks, and Billy Bob looked them straight in the eye just waiting for them to make a move. By this point they had noticed our wigs. I had a mullet wig on, Mexican Mike had a rainbow curly hair clown wig on, Chopper Bob had an afro wig on, and Billy Bob had a mop of curly hair. One of them yelled, These guys are freaks man! And they saunter off like we were wasting their time.

It was strange. Those vatos were dangerous. Billy Bob said that he's seen them type of guys all his life and they'll end up going back to jail. They will pick a fight and get knocked out and go back to jail or get killed. I said I knew the type and he was right about that.

The Pepes exchange looks. The detective says, You think Billy Bob is a stand-up guy because he was going to kill those guys?

You don't get it. Billy Bob was taking care of us. He was trying to keep me out of jail. Man, where I come from, you don't back down or else you'll be on your back the rest of your life. Billy Bob was willing to go all the way for us, and we were willing to go all the way for him. I think that's what society has all wrong. If you live by the gun, then you die by the gun. That's it. You don't put some stupid intellectual judgement on it like, well, he took too many swings at a person or one too many hits. You gonna cry about if someone gets punched in the face one too many times when you're doing battle for your life? Legally that may fly, but being legal don't make you right. Just ask the blacks pre-civil rights. What comes next? Someone can rob a gas station, commit a violent crime but then sue the gas station for using excess force?

Did you rob a gas station, Chino? Man, you're missing my point.

Did Billy Bob rob a gas station? No, that was just an example. I mean, Billy Bob did rob a gas station when he was 12. Believe it not, he stole two 12-packs of beer, just grabbed 'em and started running with 'em. It's funny to me because he loved beer even at such a young age.

I'm guessing he got away with it. No, the cops got him but drove him home and were telling him how he would be a good cop one day. Billy Bob thinks they drank his beer.

Why are you telling me this Chino? If I understood you correctly, you asked if Billy Bob robbed a gas station.

Ay! Nevermind! Have you ever been robbed? No, but Bob got robbed.

You mean Billy Bob? Yeah, Billy Bob got robbed and he beat that dude up bad then duct-taped his mouth, hands, and feet.

You're kidding me. No, I'm not kidding you. I was there. Billy Bob called the police non-emergency number, then cracked open a beer and turned up his oldies while the dude was just duct-taped up for I don't know how long till a cruiser showed up.

Billy Bob sounds like a rough character, even if he's never gone to jail for it. Look, Detective Pepe, it's not Billy Bob's fault some guy tried to mug him! And it's not my fault you were beat up in high school and your mama didn't love you. You're here trying to find reasons to lock Billy Bob up, but the funny thing is if you were just nice to him he would be your fiercest defender.

Yeah, right. Duct-taping someone's mouth isn't criminal, after all. He was cursing us out good! Billy Bob hates curse words. He warned him first, then duct-taped his mouth shut because the guy simply wouldn't shut up his cussing. Billy Bob thinks his grandma wouldn't approve of curse words. He's kind of weird that way, I guess.

Billy Bob is a former Marine sniper, EOD expert, and combat vet from Afghanistan to Iraq. He's no criminal. I love the guy. You're all high and mighty, Detective Pepe. Get off your high horse, man. You're just a systems and institution guy, good man! Get in line like the mindless drone that you are.

That's the difference between you and me, Detective Pepe.

The detective leaned forward and spat, Was it you who killed Isabella, you little bald Chinaman? Deputy Pepe grabbed his father's arm to warn him to calm down. Chino spat right back, Billy Bob was right—you're a regular Inspector Clouseau.

Where were you the night Isabella died? I was the bartender that night and the last I seen her was when she left with Jon. After work I went home and watched *Happy Days*. Potsie and Fonzie—Aayy!

Is everyone at this motel some kind of clown? Get out of my sight, Chino!

Chino goes back to the Sun Brewing Motel and tells Billy Bob, The Pepes think we're both criminals and that I killed Isabella. Don't worry Chino, Detective Pee-Pee is a nincompoop and his son is a wannabe tough guy. I think the web sleuths will find out who done it before anyone else. That Ramona and her brother, David, have been detailing and documenting everything about this case. Ramona was asking me how Isabella could have gotten into that egg fermenter long before Pepe did.

A week later, Detective Pepe comes back to the Sun Brewing Motel with the final autopsy results. He tells Billy Bob, The cause of death is inconclusive. They can't determine if she drowned before or after she entered the beer fermenter. They did find a partial DNA sequence under her nails. The murderer probably hoped dumping her in an active fermentation would clean the DNA. The case is far from closed. I'll need to take a DNA sample from everyone. Peter objects. I don't want to give my DNA to the government. I'll force each and every one of you here at this motel by court order, or you can simply give me one. The choice is yours. Peter said, Go ahead and get your court order, Detective Martinez, but until then I'm resisting. This makes you suspicious, Peter. Billy Bob says, Oh come on, Pee-Pee! He's a dwarf for crying out loud! Do you really think Peter could have carried a full-grown woman up a 10-foot egg-shaped fermenter? Maybe he's stronger than he looks. What about you, Billy Bob? I'll give my DNA. No problem, Detective. I've got nothing to hide.

Billy Bob gathers everyone on shift and announces, I have a new beer release coming out later today: Meados de Alien. We all need to start preparing. There will be a special keg tapping event this evening. Let's get going.

With the release of the official autopsy, the web sleuths are back, making their videos about who knows what, since no one is telling them anything else.

Three of them are filming with their phones and following Billy Bob while asking him stupid questions. Ramona and David are waiting for him in the bar and ask, Is it true your new release of Meados de Alien was fermenting in the same egg fermenter that Isabella was dumped in? Billy Bob says, You firken web sleuths! David asks, Why is your beer called Meados de Alien?

We've cleaned and sterilized the fermenter. It's perfectly safe. Meados de Alien is Spanish and translates in English to Alien Piss. Ramona asks another question: We now know Isabella's bed in her room was pissed in, is there a connection? Billy Bob replied, For Pete's sakes, where did you find that information? Who told you that?

Ramona keeps going: She was also from Mexico. Doesn't the name of this beer seem insensitive? Do you hate immigrants, Billy Bob?

Billy Bob shouts, Okay, I'm not doing any more interviews. I have a business to run. I've already told the police and most of you everything there is to tell. It's all on record.

Chapter 4.

Dear Diary,

It's intoxicating having an addictive personality. I guess it's a flaw of mine but it does make me feel real good.

When I look in the mirror, I'm pretty. I see someone that is beautiful, very polite and well mannered, extremely intelligent, very attractive, charismatic and eloquent—however I'm surprised a lot of people don't see it that way.

I guess it takes a special person to connect with me. Once we're connected, it's for life.

This small western town of Canutillo has turned into a circus. I never imagined a murder would turn a small dusty border-town in the middle of the desert, sitting on the Rio Grande, into a tourist destination for the Sun Brewing Motel.

The world has gone mad.

A year goes by, and Isabella's mystery is still unsolved. Time flies when you're having fun, I guess. The annual Rock 'N' Roll Halloween Costume Ball is this week. Billy Bob booked The Nobody's and Ray Monroe's band The Third Edge. Those are his favorite two local bands. He always gives preference to people he knows well.

Costume parties are the greatest; you'll see someone dressed as Bob Ross or a banana with apples.

A young woman who looks maybe 21 years of age with bleach blond hair is walking around kind of lost. Peter comes out to great her and tells her the Dallas Cowboy cheerleader tryouts are not until tomorrow. She giggles. I'm here to get one of your famous motel rooms filled wall-to-wall with beer. Peter grins his adorable elfin grin and says, You've come to the right place. What's your name? Daisy Swallow. Let's get you a room, Daisy. Peter leads her to the front desk.

I'll be staying a few days, she says. I'm a tourist on my way to Phoenix. Excellent, says Peter. You'll be here for our annual Rock 'N' Roll Halloween Costume Ball. Sounds great. That's a lovely accent you have, Daisy. You must be a southern belle. I am indeed. I'm from a small town in Louisiana. I'm just going to Phoenix to meet up with some sorority sisters for a little vacay. That's nice, Daisy. Peter hands her a room key. Well, you're all set up. Enjoy your stay. My name is Peter Francois Amador; I'll be of service to you for anything you'll need. My, that's an interesting name. What kind is it? I'm an English-French-Mexican-American and speak all three of those languages fluently. Well, aren't you adorable? Tootles, Peter Francey Amadeus. Tootl-oo, Daisy.

Daisy meanders her way to the bar and takes a beer menu from Chino. Chino's a real talker, cracking jokes and entertaining people. Daisy notices Chino has chopsticks in his hand, so naturally she asks him about it. Why are you carrying around chop sticks in your hands? Good question, Daisy. I'm a TV star, you know. Me and Billy Bob just did a film shoot with our unfiltered Cantina Lager where I play the role of Master Chino, and I capture a fly with chopsticks. Billy Bob plays my apprentice trying to catch flies with his chopsticks, but he's too distracted with his beer. Billy Bob writes short stories, and we were practicing karate before we ever opened because we were worried about people invading the place to drink up all our beer. We did a short film for the internets. Had the song "Kung Fu Fighting" playing in the background and everything. Daisy laughs and says, The name of the beer doesn't sound at all Chinese, and anyway, if I'm honest, the story sounds dumb. Chino replies, You must have Joker syndrome. Do any beers on the menu interest you? The saison does...What is a saison? Ah, yes. Saison de Membrillo is an international award-winning beer. Daisy interrupts, Oh, I meant Le Cygne Noir. Oh, that's great too. It's a black saison. It has more of a neutral flavor with a mild citrus herbal spice that is very refreshing. Although its color is black, it doesn't have the dark, roasty flavors of a typical black-colored beer like a stout because it was made with midnight wheat. Midnight wheat gives the beer its dark color without the strong flavors you get in porters or stouts. Boy, you get excited talking about beer. Lady, this beer is to die for! Then I would like to have your tallest glass of Le Cygne Noir with a slice of Billy Bob's Matcha Crepes Cake.

Daisy goes and sits at a table on the patio and is greeted by Maggie. Daisy asks her who owns the place and Maggie says, The guy in the kitchen cooking... He's an excellent chef. His name is Billy Bob. You can meet him if you order some food; he always serves his own food. It's a requirement here: Anyone who cooks, serves it themselves. That's just the way Billy Bob wants it. Okay, so will he bring out my matcha crepes cake? Maggie says, He does sometimes, depending on how swamped he is with orders. Billy Bob will always bring out the entrées. Desserts are more iffy.

Daisy picks up the menu again. Maybe I'll order an entrée, then. Then she cries out, OMG! He has pig head tacos! I won't be having that... Let's see... How about the smoked corned beef brisket sandwich? Excellent choice, says Maggie. I'll put in the order. The Key Lime pie is also a great dessert. No thanks, but I will have the grilled baba ganoush.

About halfway through her beer, Billy Bob brings her a magnificent sandwich with beer-battered onion rings and a loaf of fresh bread with baba ganoush. Daisy gets the biggest smile on her face and asks, Are you the Billy Bob I've been hearing about? Yep, that's me. The guy that smells like mesquite wood and the guy who beer battered your onion rings and made your ale. OMG, you have two different colored eyes! You don't say? Don't tease me; they're beautiful. And this sandwich smells amazing. I think I'm in love with you, Billy Bob. Billy Bob looks himself over and responds, You got to be kidding me. I have a salt-and-pepper Wolfman Jack beard, a greasy chef's coat over overalls, and this extra-large chef's toque hat. You ain't had enough to drink to love me yet. Well, I love your country accent, Billy Bob. That so? And all this time I thought I had an El Paso accent. Enjoy your food, Daisy.

Billy Bob walks away, but Daisy gets up and follows him. You want to hang out tonight, Billy Bob, just us two? You're sweet, but no, ma'am. I'm married with kids. I'm a family man! Yeah, but are you happily married, Billy Bob? Yes, I am, as a matter of fact. Hey, you don't want your food to get cold.

Daisy returns to her table. Billy Bob goes to the bar to talk to Chino. Hey, Chino, what's up with these young girls nowadays? I mean, this little girl is barely 21 years old and essentially asking me to go straight to bed with her—and I'm almost twice her age. Billy Bob, she doesn't know anything about you, bro, except you're the owner, brewer, and chef of this place. Maybe she saw this place on the news, too. A girl like that just wants your status and money. Billy Bob responds, Yeah, her and everyone else. This business makes you realize that you have no friends—even the friends you once had. Everyone just wants a piece of you, somehow. Hey, bro, that's not me. I know, Chino. You're like my only friend. We go way back, way before any of this.

Rupprecht walked up during this conversation, and now he tells Billy Bob, Don't worry, ringmaster. I love blondes. Peter now walks up and joins the conversation, too, and says, Ah, the A Team! I love it when a plan comes together. Rupprecht tells Billy Bob, Blondes only *act* ditzy because society tells them they're supposed to. If you peel away the layers, they can surprise you with how scholarly, well-informed, astute, and enlightened they are. I've always known you're obsequious Rupprecht but now you're becoming pedantic, Peter said. Rupprecht said, Nobody likes to be stereotyped or pigeon-holed; give her a chance and for her I am the very definition of obsequious!

Billy Bob responds, Rupprecht, If I'm the ringmaster of this circus, then do me a favor and start acting like a good juggler. That's what I really am. I'm dressed as a clown and I juggle all day. But seriously, I think Daisy would be blown away with your wealth of knowledge and your big words, Rupprecht. Peter tells Billy Bob, Oh, I think you're a liar, boss. Peter, help me out here. As you wish, ringmaster—don't be a paraquat. A what, now, Peter? Peter answers, There are hidden beauties and pleasures in sunflowers, Billy Bob.

Billy Bob moves on and asks Rupprecht, How's the Monster's Bride Ale coming along? The spunding is finished and it's pure excellence, Billy Bob. Though it's not dramatically different than Frankenstein. What about Canutillo Hoppy Vampires' Brew? That beer is a gold medal, pure perfection. Ah, ah, there's no such thing as perfection! And how's the Dark Elf Ale? Rupprecht answers, You brewed that one, Billy Bob. I'll go taste the beers soon and evaluate all of them. Good. I want them Halloween beers triple gold,

Rupprecht! And be sure Jon is becoming as skilled as you. We are only as strong as our weakest link in the team.

Jeez Laweez, Chino, it takes talent dealing with all these personalities, Billy Bob says when Rupprecht and Peter have left. Chino responds, Especially yours, Billy Bob. Billy Bob wasn't sure how to take that. What's that? You're the most interesting man in the world, Billy Bob. It stirs up strong reactions in people. What in the world are you talking about, Chino? I'm just firken with ya, Billy Bob. Just joshing around. Chino, you've finally started picking up words that aren't curse words. You got that bottle of mezcal hidden under the bar? Chino replies, You know I do. Billy Bob tells Chino, Let's have a shot, then. I've never been much of a liquor drinker, but mezcal is my favorite.

Speaking of firkin, Billy Bob continues, growing chatty, we'll be ready to crack another one in a couple days. I love the October firkins. This is my favorite time of year, Chino. Autumn is mystical, the season changing, the leaves rustling in the breeze, turning colors, and the weather perfect for brewing spontaneous ales. I'm looking forward to this year's batch of 100% spontaneous ales. Chino tipped his glass toward his boss. You know, Billy Bob, some people are still weirded out by your spontaneous fermentation tanks because of what happened to Isabella. Billy Bob replies, On a scientific level, we have powerful acidic sanitizers, but one could imagine how people would see Isabella sort of haunting our beers. Chino says, You brewed Meados de Alien in the same fermentation tank, but that beer isn't a 100 percent spontaneous ale. Why did you do that, Billy Bob? Most people don't know that, Chino. I was running out of fermenters, and Meados de Alien is really a fruited wild ale with a saison yeast strain. Chino asks, So it's a mixed-culture beer? Yeah, you could say that. We opened the kettle up to make it a wild ale by introducing it to the microbes from the air. I then let it ferment a little bit a day or two. Finally I boil it to kill the wildies, then pitch a cultured saison yeast strain that takes it from there. But that one fermenter is over 20 thousand dollars. No way am I retiring it.

Chino says, Aye... Billy Bob, this makes me remember when me, you, and your wife ran this business, just us three. You taught me how to brew, and we did it out of buckets. Billy Bob says, Good times, Chino. My wife was an excellent brewer, too. I taught her the esoteric ways of brewing, and she taught me how to cook her family-style Mexican food. You, Chino, were my shelter from everyone. I'm not exactly a front-end guy. People loved me or hated me. You and my wife really ran the front end well while I brewed or cooked. Good memories. What's amazing to me, Chino, is how you're a throwback from the 60s but have exceptional people skills that feel very current. You're older than me, for crying out loud. I love that you're tough as nails, Chino. You would have made a great Marine. You saved me many times from pouting over a bad review or from simply shoving a customer's face in my German beer chocolate cake. I guess personality goes a long ways.

Honestly, Billy Bob, I've never met someone like you. You're seriously crazy, like you're from another planet. Billy Bob responds, We are all off in some ways, bro. You want to know crazy? I remember you running out of gas on your bike, and we pulled over, then you pull out some of your moonshine and took a swig of it. You lit the air on fire with your breath. It smelled like pure gasoline. I've tasted your moonshine, Chino. It's not bad at times, but you got to be careful. You mess moonshine up with even the smallest bit of methane and you've lost your eyesight or worse. But I loved your genius idea: Take one last huge swig, then pour it straight into your gas tank. It worked to get your bike started up, but I'm glad you didn't kill yourself. The dinner crowd starts to arrive. Chino says, Thanks for the good conversation, Billy Bob.

The Rock 'N' Roll Halloween Costume Ball was always a big party at the Sun Brewing Motel. Billy Bob, dressed as Frankenstein, starts the day off by playing classic Halloween music like "Monster Mash" and "Purple People Eater" by Bobby Pickett and The Crypt Kickers, then maybe a little "Thriller" by Michael Jackson, then he'll start to gradually increase the tone to "Don't Fear the Reaper" by Blue Oyster Cult, then finally to metal songs like Rob Zombie's "American Witch." He paired Halloween music with Halloween beers and his Halloween cuisine such as Billy Bob's Frankenstein and Vampire cookies and Witches' Bread Fingers with Ghoulish Dip.

Daisy is starting early. Chino gives her some table lager because the day has just begun. Meados de Alien tends to knock people out early, and Frankenstein is so strong it's one and done. Daisy is running around dressed as Cinderella and is all smiles. She makes her way to the patio area and asks for Billy Bob to serve her. Maggie told her, He's cooking his Halloween concoctions, but he'll bring you some food if you order. Okay, then I'll order the Witches' Fingers with Ghoulish Dip. Can I also have a glass of Meados de Alien? Moments later, Billy Bob comes out with the food and tells her, If you want something a little more savory, I have my Vampire Bat Ears in Frankenstein Barbecue Sauce. I also have Vampiro Tacos or my Werewolf Burger. OMG! What are vampire bat ears? They are smoked barbecued pig ears on indirect heat so that they are tender but crisp on the outside and caramelized from my Frankenstein BBQ sauce. That sounds interesting, Billy Bob, but I'm afraid enough of your Witches' Fingers just by looking at them. I can't imagine your vampire bat ears. That's just fine, Daisy. Billy Bob, I'm your Cinderella, and I'm all yours. I don't think Cinderella and

Frankenstein would make a good match. Oh, I don't know. Look, Daisy, I'm a monster. It was a conscious decision; at least I know what I am. My wife is the monster's bride. You're better off with that guy over there, Superman. Bon Appetit.

Daisy downed the rest of her Meados and called over Maggie. What do you recommend next? I like the Werewolf from Helles lager. I think I'd like a Frankenstein Ale. Actually, may I have a couple bottles of that Frankenstein to take to my room? Of course, I'll be right back—or do you want them delivered to your room? Have Billy Bob deliver them, please. I need to get my beauty rest. I'll see what I can do, dearie.

Everywhere you look you see people in costumes roaming around the patio. The minister came as a Trooper Elvis and is performing real weddings over by the river. The last couple Trooper Elvis married had just gotten matching tattoos from across the street at Rivertrail Studios by the legendary tattoo artist, David Ibarra. Ibarra is an artistical genius who has an insane gift for artwork especially drawing and painting. Impulse tattoos, full motel rooms, flowing beer, yummy food, and getting married are commonplace for this extravaganza of an event at The Sun Brewing Motel.

As the day turns to night and the local rock bands are playing, people are having the time of their lives. The night winds down, people are about done and wandering about. They always wander to the back of the motel on the railroad tracks and to the river—especially the love birds who like to kissy kiss in the dark under the weeping willow tree.

At closing time, people are still lingering and trying to sober up. The bands are done playing and they've switched to a playlist. Another couple sneaks out to the willow tree at the back of the motel. Over the speakers we hear The Misfits' "Dig up them Bones." The couple starts making out by the tree, and soon enough it's starting to get a little heavy. They kind of swing around the tree, backing up a bit, but then they hit something hanging from the tree. We can hear the girl scream from the patio. A few of us run down there and see a woman dressed as Cinderella hanging by her feet. The girl is weeping, now, and the guy is trying to comfort her while everyone gathers round and wonders what to do.

Eventually, the police show up. All the witnesses are sitting on the patio not knowing what to say. The last man to show up is Detective Pepe. The crime scene would be hard to mess up this time because all you have is a person tied by her feet with old-fashioned boat rope and hanging from a tree.

The police secured the area, looking for evidence under huge floodlights. They try to record all the footprints, but probably a dozen of us had been down there tramping about so it's not likely they'll find much that way. They finished up taking their notes and people's statements and went away feeling perplexed.

Nobody had seen or heard anything unusual that night.

Chapter 5.

Dear Diary,

It's not every day you see a girl dressed as Cinderella hanging by her feet from a tree.

What kind of a lunatic would go to that kind of trouble?

I was pleased to meet her—I'm a connoisseur. People would consider me the devil in disguise, a real monster but I would hope people see me as having a sense of humor too. It was a little comical seeing Cinderella hanging upside down. Another way to look at it is the way a lion looks at a gazelle. It's appetite—or maybe my appetite comes from something else? She was prey in a sense but it's more like her kind are dodo birds bound for extinction.

It was time for a change and she didn't know the nature of the medium of my exchange.

It's funny how things work out. You could've been the greatest architect, meticulous or turned sloppy but not predetermined. I give people a choice in life, to choose. It's only fair. Unfortunately, the dodo didn't adapt.

I told Daisy, Now that we're getting to know each other, I have a serious question for you: Why would Cinderella be a rotten date?

Daisy was thrown off and agitated.

But I don't let her off the hook. Just answer, please. Then she said something very amusing... She said, It's time for me to blow this popsicle stand!

I said politely, The answer is: She limps when she walks on her one high heel, she runs away from the party too early, and she smells like pumpkin.

This really irked her because she resorted to insulting me. She said, That's not even funny, and anyway your costume looks ridiculous! Some gentleman you are. Get me alone and tell me I'm a rotten date.

Daisy's interpretation is somewhat an accurate way to look it, I was just curious and wanted her to entertain me for a few seconds.

What is it with people nowadays? They're really lacking—thin skinned and very rude. I told her something very important, that I always tell people.

Grandma always said, If you can't say something nice, then don't say anything at all.

How close are you to your grandma?

She ignored my serious question.

I was very close to my grandma, and I was her favorite.

Things didn't go too well with Daisy, not even after our interesting conversations and my killer wit.

Maybe it's me... Maybe it's my dark triad of traits or my gray matter? Maybe I should meditate and start fasting but when I do that, I realize I'm the person I want to be... hungry and hell-bent. Fasting also makes me walk around with a mirror looking at myself to see if my complexion has changed. I would also like to walk around the mall looking at myself with a mirror, too, but I wouldn't want people staring at me, so I don't. I am self-conscious and an introspective person after all.

Detective Pepe needs a break in the case somehow. Two murders in a 15 months at the same property. He has nothing, not a clue, except a note that is of burned antique paper written in calligraphy tied with thin rope around her right hand that read:

Daisies follow the Sun.

Daisies dancing in the Rain.
Daisy the lonesome Dove with so much Pain.
Too many lonesome Doves all the same.
Daisy the fairy tale not in vain.
You're no Daisy.

Billy Bob told Detective Pepe that he thinks The Sun Brewing Motel is getting set up somehow; he is devastated by it all. Maybe it's those vicious web sleuths, he suggests, trying to fabricate a story. Or it could be transients, too. This place is a crossroads for a lot of different people coming and going.

It's getting close to Thanksgiving, which is Billy Bob's favorite holiday. He puts every TV in the pub on Cornhusker football. We always wondered why he's so fanatical about Husker football, and we would ask him what gives, and he would always reply with a different answer. This time he responds, Ah, shucks, fellas. I love to wear my cone-shaped corn hat for Thanksgiving, is all. But he knows every player and all the history of the Nebraska Cornhuskers. Another one of Billy Bob's quirks.

Detective Pepe and his posse are starting to make regular visits for Billy Bob's beer donuts and to watch football. Pepe, Sr. always complains he has to watch the Cornhuskers; Pepe, Jr. only talks when he has something rude to say to someone. This time they are in luck because the detective has figured out to come after the Husker game and when Billy Bob has his beer-injected turkey with his wife's stuffing on the menu. It's to die for—and afterward there's pumpkin pie!

Billy Bob leans against the bar talking to Chino. How do we know it's not Detective Pepe who is the killer? he says. What are you, loco? says Chino. More likely Deputy Pepe; that hombre's a dark dude. But why would a lawman do something like that? I dunno. Maybe his mama didn't give him enough attention growing up. And he'd know how to leave clues to draw attention away from him. Meanwhile he gets to hang out here eating free donuts.

He can sure put away the pumpkin beer, says Chino. Billy Bob says, I guess there is no law for drinking while riding a horse.

Come springtime, Billy Bob holds his annual Keg Party on the Rio, which is an organic craft beer festival behind the motel right on the banks of the Rio Grande. Anyone can take part: local farmers selling their fruits and vegetables, food trucks, arts and crafts booths. There's also festivities like the river raft race, which requires contestants to down a Sun Brewing six pack before they cross the finish line. Ray Monroe's band plays every year later in the afternoon. He and his long time band mate, Sam Dayoub comprise of the main musicians of their band, The Third Edge, but he also has a lot of side gigs with new names like Green Light Go or Ray Monroe and the Crickets—or was it The Mad Hatters? All the names over the years are a blur, but they are always extremely talented and always perform good music. Billy Bob goes all out for this event, he even has the KLAQ Buzz Adams morning show live then followed by Mike G and The Jukebox on the Fox for the rest of the day. He barbecues an entire pig each and every year. This single event attracts the most people and takes a lot of work from everyone, but it's always good times.

Billy Bob's in-laws all come out, including Mary (Margarita's sister-in-law), Mary's dad, Rigoberto Del Toro and her extensive side of the family fill up the patio for a bite to eat and some brews to drink. They love to eat, like a starving army traveling on foot in the harshest of conditions. Billy Bob's special of the day is his family style mole. Mary and Rigoberto order Billy Bob's mole with a Mademoiselles Helles lager, a traditional German lager. Billy Bob brings out the food and says, Surprise! which doesn't make any sense but amuses the younger kids.

Billy Bob returns to the kitchen while Rigoberto starts eating the mole, but something is wrong. He signals to Maggie and aks her to bring Billy Bob back out here. Billy Bob returns to see what's going on, and Rigoberto told him, This isn't mole, take it away. He goes on to say, You shouldn't be cooking Mexican food. You don't know what you're doing! That was the worst plate of mole in recorded history. He said it loud and proud in front of everyone on the patio. You're supposed to be some great brewer too? This isn't a German lager! I know German beer.

Billy Bob usually walks away muttering if he gets too upset, but this time he really let Rigoberto have it. He said, Hey, don't you ever embarrass me or my staff this way again, you tuerto! That is my grandma's mole—it's my family tradition. You loudmouth schnook! And that is a classic German-style helles lager crafted in the same manner as they do in the old world using old-world techniques like a decoction mash and an acid rest which improves clarity and head retention, not that you'd know the difference. The beta enzyme cuts through the proteins into higher molecular weight fragments. Precision pH of 5.3, mashed out at 169 degrees for 15 minutes. Fermented precisely at 50 degrees Fahrenheit with German lager yeast. You know German beer? You're full of kaka de toro!

Rigoberto stands up and shouts back, Don't you talk to me that way, young man! No one talks to Rigoberto Del Toro that way! Billy Bob doubles down: You're Rigoberto Kaka de Toro! You will always be Rigoberto Kaka de Toro to me! Billy Bob storms off muttering corksucker, firkin sassafras—then marches back to say, That's not your cheap macro-brewed lager, sir. It's my craft German lager!

Rupprecht and Chino are watching from the doorway. He's right, you know, says Rupprecht. That's a true German lager. I showed Billy Bob how to make it in the European way. Chino says, The old man knows how to press Billy Bob's buttons, that's all. Those two fight like cats and dogs. It's tough to hear criticism, Rupprecht says. Chino responds, This is a tough business we are in, Rupprecht.

Maggie walks up and throws a rag on the bar. Billy Bob really lost it this time, she says. Rupprecht says, I appreciate that about Billy Bob—he's passionate. I can't remember the last time I was so enraged. Maggie replied, Rupprecht, you're the very definition of a machine—always cool, calm, and collected. Chino chimes in and says, It's always the quiet ones—calm, cool, and collected—who are psychos and surprise everyone. Maggie laughs and says, You saying our Ruppee, here, is the big bad murderer? Naw, says Chino. He's probably just a pervert.

If you ask me, Chino, Billy Bob is the psycho, Rupprecht says. If he doesn't calm down he's going to start taking it out on everyone. Chino said pointedly, Stop complaining. He's not paying you to talk behind his back. Go get some work done. I've done plenty of good work, young man. Rupprecht replied. I've taught Billy Bob the old and ancient ways of brewing in the German/European tradition. Yes, you did, Rupprecht, and yet he is a better brewer than you. You're an idiot, Chino, but at least you're loyal. I guess the judges for the world's most prestigious beer competitions are idiots, too? When was the last time you won an international award for your beer Rupprecht? Rupprecht walks away. Chino calls after him, Enough said; I rest my case. These new generations are ingrates. I need another shot of mezcal.

Billy Bob was so disturbed he walked down to the river. He looks into the sky and starts talking to his grandma. After that he calls his wife. Margarita answers and Billy Bob tells her, You got a messed up family Margarita! I can't believe they did this to me. I can't believe I talked to an old man like that either. I lost my cool, I hate it when I do that. I feel bad afterwards. We are always so nice to them, all of them, and always going out of our way for Mary and Rigoberto. I've never seen such gossiping and entitlement. They are spoiled rotten people, and at that age... For the love of all that is holy, you're supposed to gain wisdom as you get older. Margarita replies, Don't worry Billy Bob, you're the type of guy people love or hate, very little in-between. Just come home and lay on the sofa and we'll talk about it over another therapy session, my love. Billy Bob says, Are you eating hot Cheetos while you're talking to me? Margarita replies, How'd you know? Geez amor, I've never seen someone love hot Cheetos so much. I can hear you munching on them. You know, Margarita, you're my little hot tamale. I love my little talks with my little smoochie-poo. You're my sugar-boo.

Okay, calm down over there, Margarita says. I already talked to Mary. All she did was complain and tell me how you called her Dad a tuerto. Yeah, well, says Billy Bob, he does have a crazy eye. Mary and Rigoberto are going to be in the area tomorrow again to go to the Canutillo flea market. They invited me, but of course I declined. They bring out the worst in people. Margarita, I just hope they stay away from my family, my business, and myself.

Margarita also tells Billy Bob, You know something strange? Billy Bob replies, Yeah, a lot, recently. Which strange do you mean? Margarita says, The other day, Rigoberto and Mary were at the flea market and ran into Maggie buying turquoise jewelry from our cousin's little Tigua Indian jewelry shop. When Maggie left, Holy told them she was acting strange. Like, asking a lot of questions and taking notes. Billy Bob responds, Maggie is always like that. I can see how that seems strange to your family, but she means no harm. Sure, but who takes notes in a jewelry shop? Maybe she's comparison shopping, I don't know. Maggie is just a little eccentric, but I love her as a Sun Brewing Motel employee and friend. Margarita responds, Yeah, I guess you're right. It's probably nothing.

It's time for the annual Keg Party on the Rio. Billy Bob has been barbecuing his pig low and slow for 24 hours right on the riverbanks of the Rio Grande. Boats are floating up to grab some cans of beer, Tury is selling his local farm fresh fruits and vegetables, the shaved ice truck is camped out, Ray Monroe is setting up for an acoustical performance along with Serge Franco and his father setting up on the other side of the festival for mariachis. Ben the local artist has his paintings on display along with David Ibarra. Billy Bob has an entire grill dedicated to beer brats, smoked sausages, and hotdogs for people that want to eat something quick. He doesn't serve up the pig until after the drunken river-raft race. People are starting to show up, things are coming together.

I don't know how Billy Bob does it, but he can drink and barbecue all day long and stay functional. He must sweat it out. They say the Ancient Egyptians used beer as currency and as a food source for slave labor. Either they were drunk all the time or Billy Bob and King Tut have something special in common. Billy Bob likes to say, When I'm dranken my own beer and barbecuen, it's like I'm fixed and at one with the universe.

From out back of the bar you can just see the contestants lined up about 300 yards up river. Peter fires the flare gun to start the raft race. Rafts decorated like Mario Bros. and Lady Gaga and Stranger Things madly paddle off the starting line. All they have to do is down a six-pack of lager and cross the finish line first. You can split the beers or give them all to one person; it doesn't matter. There's cheering and screaming and someone has a horn of some kind. Super Mario finishes first. Everyone cheers for the DJ from El Paso's legendary local rock station KLAQ. Super Mario sure can chuggle beer and move fast for a big guy. He finished first and drank the entire 6 pack and belched so loud it echoed down the river.

Chino is in his homemade raft made from scrap wood from his tool shed and is slowly coming down the riverbanks without a worry in the world. He must have been secretly taking swigs of mezcal. He's stuck a little ways up from the finish line. Chino gets out and starts waving his hands and yelling at us all to come over there. People start gathering around to see what's going on. Billy Bob yelled, Jeepers! People become frantic and take off running and making phone calls. There are two bodies tied up with rope fastened to cement blocks. Their heads are just below the surface.

Detective Pepe and his posse show up to investigate. Some people are not even phased by this; they just want more beer. Billy Bob closes everything down and asks people to leave. A lot of people are not really leaving, though. Some are just scared and want to know what's going on. Others are holding their phones and recording everything.

It looks like Detective Pepe really means business this time. He showed up relatively quick and not on a horse. He brought re-inforcements. The police are blockading the area. Looks like special teams are here to evaluate.

When they pull up the bodies, they find an old green Grolsch bottle tied around both their hands. There's a message inside.

In the aftermath, Pepe still doesn't seem to have a clue what is going on around here with all these victims. Detective Pepe questions each and every one from the motel and it seems everyone has an alibi. Billy Bob was in a beer induced snoring rage all night according to his wife. Maggie was home sleeping over with her parents. Jon and Rupprecht went out together and stayed in the city Truth or Consequences, New Mexico. Peter worked the grave-yard shift at the motel.

Peter ponders the question and says, Who's to say these two were in the river tied up last night? I guess Detective Pepe will uncover more clues with the post mortem analysis. I'm sure they'll identify who these two people are, how long they've been in the river, and when they were last seen.

Detective Pepe comes by the Sun Brewing Motel a few days later and tells Billy Bob and others listening around, We believe we've identified the two bodies but it won't be official until the conclusion of the autopsy. Peter notices Ramona and her brother David approaching with a video recorder. Billy Bob and Peter go outside to talk to them. David tells Billy Bob, We know it's you! with his cute accent. Peter says, Why would you say a thing like that, David? Ramona tells them, I've been following every detail of these murders. I'm not just covering this for sensationalism but for justice for our community. We've got our eyes on you, Billy Bob. And don't think about moving against me; I intend to turn everything I have over to the police. Anything happens to me and they'll know it was you in a heartbeat. Billy Bob hands her a box of donuts and says, I know I'm a murderous monster and all, but I brought you these donuts. Feel free to come back for more if you ever decide I'm not going to kill you.

All the web sleuths are going crazy over these new bodies and already putting out their theories about the identities of the victims. Ramona is the most cautious, but even she says she believes the two victims are Mary and Rigoberto Del Toro. In fact, Margarita hasn't heard from her sister-in-law or Mary's father and can't find any sign of them, so she begins to worry they're right.

Billy Bob grows increasingly agitated by the day as he hears more and more theories. He asks people not to talk to him about it, but Chino can't help letting him know what people are saying. He yells out to no one in particular, Those amateur Web sleuths!

They think they know everything! I just lost my cool and for good firkin reason, and now I'm murdering my own family? No judge, no jury, straight to execution! That's your web sleuth amateur justice. Whatever gets more likes or links or whatever. I work my tail off for this community! ...I built this business one beer at a time! It's just not fair!

Detective Pepe's investigation turns up few useful clues, but he does invite Margarita down to the mortuary. Billy Bob goes with her. Some time later they come out again and Margarita is an inconsolable mess of tears. The victims were, in fact, Mary and Rigoberto Del Toro.

Some time later Det. Pepe returns to the motel and sits at the bar. Billy Bob comes out to greet him, and the detective suggests it would be best if they talk alone. There's nothing you can't say in front of Chino. Have it your way. I'm sorry about your in-laws, Billy Bob. I hear you didn't get on with them, but that don't mean much when it comes to murder. Thank you, detective. But something's been bothering me about the way we found them. There's something very peculiar about it all. I'd say, says Chino. They were tied to cement blocks in the river. It wasn't that. First of all, it appears they had been injected with a deadly venom of some kind, probably scorpion. The kind you get on the black market. Second, and possibly related, there was a green beer bottle tied to Mary's left hand and Rigoberto's right hand. Inside the bottle was a scorpion and a note written in calligraphy on paper that had been burned at the edges like someone was trying to make it look older than it was. That's different than the other murders, Chino says. That's right, it is. Well, what did this note say? asks Billy Bob. The detective pulled out his notebook and flipped to a certain page and began to read:

I hope you guess my name.

I've been around for a great many years in this business.

I've been around the world many times from Saint Petersburg to Rio and now to Canutillo.

From sinners, your taste has always been taint.

To saints, I've tried to show some restraint.

In this river there is no coming back.

I'm not a maniac and this isn't payback.

I like playing the harp and I had a hamster named McLoven.

Well, what the hell does that mean? asks Chino. Something, maybe, says Pepe. Or maybe nothing. Maybe it's an elaborate ruse of some kind, or the incoherent ravings of a madman. But you don't think that, do you? says Billy Bob. Nope, says Pepe. What do you think, then?

I think he wants to get caught.

{ 6 }

Chapter 6.

Dear Diary,

I have many diaries but this one is my favorite. I believe I'll call it—My Murder Diary. At first, I wasn't sure if I should give my diary a catchy name about all the people I've helped but I think that now it's appropriate after all these murders. I actually saved them—however thankless they are—and I gave them a good beer and meal.

Maybe I'll be famous one day because of my unique taste but I'm already rich. As a person of taste, having style goes hand in hand after all.

Detective Pepe is a big dummy with limited capacities—he'll never catch me. I'm way too foxy for him.

The Sun Brewing Motel has just received national attention for these murders and the authorities haven't a clue. I imagine the heat will get turned up a notch or two with the investigations but it'll go nowhere fast unless they bring in a renowned detective.

They probably consider me a big bad wolf but it's really because I don't play by society's silly rules that seem to change for the privileged.

On a hot, sunny afternoon, Leopold Wienke, Texas Ranger, pulls up to the Sun Brewing Motel. He steps out of his car and looks like he learned how to be a ranger by watching TV: jeans, a mustache, dark glasses, white hat. A smaller, Tejano man steps out of the passenger side. He's also got jeans and dark glasses, but his mustache is pencil-thin and he wears no hat. A few web sleuths who have been camping out in front of the motel get out their cameras, but Wienke gives them a look to let them know to keep their distance.

Peter greets the men then takes them to Billy Bob in the bar. Billy Bob greets them and says, Pleased to meet you, Mr. Wiener-Key. It's pronounced Win-Kay. Oh, I guess I got it confused with the wieners I serve out of my cart out on the patio there. That's real cute, Billy Bob. Mr. Wien-Key, are you here to take my money? No, sir, I'm not. I'm a Texas Ranger here to investigate the deaths of Mary and Rigoberto Del Toro and their possible relation to the deaths of Daisy Swallows and Isabella Mata. Me and my trusty scribe John John Coffee are here to catch a killer, and that we will do swiftly and decisively. Chino asks, Why do they call you John John? You hard of hearing or something and they got say everything twice? John John spat on the floor. My mother named me after my father and my grandfather and always called me by my first and middle names, he says. You like to say something about my mother? Chino turns to Billy Bob and says, His mom called him by his first and middle name. Billy Bob replies, It's the Coffee part that interests me, but I'll call him John John to avoid confusion. We drink a lot of coffee around here, among other things. Can I get you guys some iced tea?

Obliged, says Wienke. Then if you don't mind, will you please bring everyone into the restaurant here so that I can talk to them. Then do you mind if John John and I use your office to talk to them individually? Sure thing, Leopold.

Billy Bob walks off with Peter, muttering, I don't like these gull dern Texas Rangers at all. Why's that, Billy Bob? Them Texas Rangers are only after the glory and to look good. I see, that does pose a problem. Yep, it poses a very big problem because they could pin this crap on me just to look like they got the bad guy and become big heroes and get their story in the papers. It's all about looking good and closing a case with these turkeys. The public will believe whatever these cowboys tell them to. Well, let's hope the Rangers don't pick on you, Billy Bob. Thanks, Peter, or on a little guy like you. That would actually be funny, Billy Bob. Those big bad tough super rangers wouldn't look so tough collaring a little person. Don't be so sure, Peter. They learn how you romance the customers with your killer charm and your preternatural strength and speed, they'll make a nice little scandal out of you. They'll have to catch me first, boss. Atta boy. Go gather everyone up for me, will ya?

Is everyone here, Billy Bob? Everyone who's here is here, Leopold. Great. For those of you who don't know who I am, I'm Lt. Wienke, Texas Ranger. Me and Officer Coffee here are going to look into your little murder problem. Jon cries out, Hey, is that one of those slick hats you get in the Flying J Travel Plaza? I always wondered who wore those.

Wienke ignored him. I have a dossier on each and every one of you here today. I know everything. Jon replies, Even Billy Bob's flatulence schedule? Billy Bob adds, We pass a lot of CO_2 in our fermentation rooms and sometimes have to burp our tanks. Mr. Wienke says, Jon, I know an awful lot of uncomfortable information about you, son. Jon responds, Like you could be my dad, Mr. Wienke? The fellas are sure gonna be impressed with me if my pa's a Texas Wrangler. Jon, I can't decide if I should put you under a hot lamp right now or let you sweat it out in here all afternoon to be the last to go. The longer I'm sitting here the more I get to drink, sir, so take your pick. Alright, let's go, Seinfeld. You'll be first.

In Billy Bob's office Ranger Wienke really did point the desk lamp at Jon. He pulled out a recorder and turned it on. This is Texas Ranger Leopold Wienke accompanied by my scribe John John Coffee. It's... He quick pulled out his phone, found the date, and spoke it into the recorder. We are here with Jon Miguel Baio, brewer at the Sun Brewing Motel. Mr. Baio, tell us about the day Mary and Rigoberto Del Toro came to The Sun Brewing Motel. Sure. I was brewing a batch of our Beauregard Ice Dark Lager that day, so I was working in the brewhouse.

That's a very particular memory you have there, Mr. Baio. It's a very particular line of work, sir. So, you weren't out on the patio when Mary and Rigoberto were dining? No, I never seen them. I only heard about the fiasco later.

What did you hear about the fiasco? Just that Rigoberto insulted Billy Bob and made a scene in front of the other customers. And Billy Bob took offense and flipped out on them. It's not the worst family spat we've had on our patio, believe me.

How did Billy Bob flip out on them? Well, everyone was talking about how Billy Bob didn't take no crap from them and put them in their place. I don't know the exact words or specifics, just that Billy Bob raised his voice and got angry and put them in their place.

Billy Bob sounds like a bit of a hothead, huh. Billy Bob? I don't know. He is a very outspoken and opinionated person, but for the most part he keeps himself in check. Billy Bob's weakness is if you insult his beer or his food. That is a sure-fire way to get under his skin. For the most part, he'll keep his cool, but sometimes he will let the customers have it. I've seen him make a spectacle when customers have insulted his cuisine. You can find it online. People think it's funny. They record it when he goes berserker on people. Some folks come just to see if there'll be fireworks that night. You have a lot of "fireworks," then? No, not really. Once in a blue moon.

Do you think Billy Bob was involved with Mary's and Rigoberto's deaths? No way, sir. Billy Bob isn't someone to mess with, but he would never murder customers, much less family, because of their bad taste buds.

Why do you say Billy Bob isn't someone to mess with? First off, he is a former Marine sniper and EOD expert. You got to have a screw loose to be that. People who truly know Billy Bob fear him.

You're making a real strong case for his innocence, Jon. He *is* innocent, so why hide the truth? That's a fine way to look at it, son. Now, why would people fear Billy Bob? He's fiercely loyal, but he has a screw loose, you know? He also has PTSD. What makes you say that? Because I have PTSD. It's something you can spot if you know what to look for. That right? Yeah, it's hard to explain. It's like an emptiness that can never be filled or a cut that never heals. There's like this darkness in the center of a person. There a darkness in you, Jon? Yes, sir, there is. And in Billy Bob? Billy Bob is carrying a lot of pain. We're a lot alike that way.

Jon Miguel Baio, I'm well aware that you're a former Navy Seal. You are a very decorated military man. By all accounts you could have had a very successful military career. What made you leave? What turned you into a drifter? Man, I just told you, I got major tweaked out there. I needed to decompress a bit and attempt to salvage what's left of my soul.

There's one thing that I don't understand, Jon. Not only do I have a dossier on you, but I've been watching you for some time now. You dress as a female and live a dual life. You go to these homo clubs dressed as a drag queen and you don't even have the common courtesy to shave your horseshoe mustache off. Does anyone know about this, Jon? No. No one knows about that, Lt. Wienke. Please don't tell anyone. That's my private life.

How does that work, Jon? I mean, are you a homosexual or do you just like dressing up like a girl and going to glamour shots? I honestly don't know. Well, you must know something. If you really must know, I've always dated women and was going to get married when I first joined the Navy. She ended up with what seems like every man on base while I was deployed. I started dating this new gal from Los Angeles. I didn't know at the time she was an amateur porn star, and she was heavy into drugs. We did a lot of drugs together—all kind of drugs, even heroin. She wasn't just an amateur porn star, she was also bisexual. She would want me to dress like a girl and I would do it for her. Next thing I know, she's taking pictures of me dressed like a girl ready for glamour shots and all high as a kite. Then she spread all those pictures to everyone I knew and all her friends. She would say, Look at my Navy Seal. It was like a badge of honor for her.

The strangest thing happened to me from then on out. I stopped caring and I let go. I wanted to be with her, and she was the worst and the best thing for me all at the same time. I kept going back to her, over and over again like a bad addiction. I left other women over spilt milk but with her it was different. I kind of became a new person.

When we split up, it was tough. I was heartbroken, but she didn't want anything to do with me anymore. So I left town for a new start.

Well, Jon, hopefully you don't have Broken Heart Syndrome. Jon replies, Yeah, I know your heart bleeds for me. At any rate, Jon, that's strange. I've never known someone who was straight that turned homo. It's more like I like to dress in women's clothing and perform. Maybe I'm bisexual part time, I don't know. Normally I'm straight.

Do you watch midget porn, Jon? What's wrong with you, man? I've answered all your questions and you come at me with that garbage. I expected more out of a Texas Ranger.

I'm all for the LGBTQ+ alphabet community, Jon. There's nothing illegal you done, but I'd prefer for the queers to stay in California, is all. No offense intended, Jon. I hope you understand. Did you know there's no homos in Texas? Once in a while homos like you pop up, but we get rid of them. You got friends out of state somewhere, Jon? I'd like to go, sir, Jon states coldly. Wienke chuckles and tells him, Oh, don't be sore. Sometimes I press the limits a bit to see how you'll handle it. Am I free to go? Are you nervous about something, Mr. Baio? Jon looked like he could bit the Ranger's face off, but he held it together and simply stared back at him.

That will be all for today, Mr. Baio. We'll be in touch. Jon rose to leave.

Oh, one last question, Jon. You mentioned you and Billy Bob are a lot alike. You live a dual life, Jon, and keep secrets from everyone. What secrets you suppose Billy Bob is keeping?

You said it yourself, lieutenant. You know everything.

Wienke follows Jon out and John John follows Wienke. Wienke signals to Billy Bob. Let's you and me go for a walk around this motel of yours. Take me to the fermenter that Isabella Mata was found in. That'd be over here on the patio, sir. It was this concrete egg fermenter right here. Wienke examines the fermenters. Half a dozen web sleuths stand with their cameras about 20 feet away.

How could someone possibly get inside one of these fermenters, Billy Bob? There's this door down here when they're empty, but we use one of these scaffold ladders on wheels to access the top hatch. You keep these scaffold ladders locked up at night? That's right. Was there any sign that someone had cut the lock that night? No, sir. So, one could conclude that whoever put Isabella in the fermenter had a key to the ladders. I wouldn't go that far, only because we've left them out before. It could have been a fluke. But, normally, yes that's correct. That's how we open the fermenter up and clean it.

Take me to the room Daisy Swallows was in. Easy enough; the rooms are just here off the patio. John John, are you getting all this? Yes, sir, lieutenant. Someone stayed the night in that room, though. Do you mind coming back after checkout? Not a problem. Take me to the tree Daisy was hanging from. Billy Bob led them off the patio and down the path to the river side, then down a little farther to the giant willow tree. Which branch was she hanging from? I believe it was this one here. Billy Bob, what I find interesting was, first, the killer used boat rope to tie her up, and second, he was brazen enough to do it with people around up on the patio there. And people was hanging out down here by the river, too, sir. Wienke looked up, down, and all around. How do you figure he did it without getting seen, then? Well, one thing, sir, the light don't quite reach down here. You can see the patio, but from up there the tree is just a dark blotch at night. There wasn't much moon, either. So he coulda been real fast.

That's right. Or he could have already been in the tree with the girl before people started wandering down here. And maybe he crawled out along that long branch over there and dropped down in the confusion without anyone noticing. I suppose he could have, yeah.

Now, Billy Bob, how many people you know know how to use boat rope and tie a proper noose and slip knot? You want me to look that up in everyone's employment files? I haven't the foggiest Wiener-Key. Jon would. I would. There's lots of people spend time on the river out here, though. And I suppose anyone could google a thing. You use boat rope in the brewery? We have in the past to jerry-rig a thing or two. There might be some lying around. We'll get to that later.

Take me to the river where Mary and Rigoberto were found. That's just right over there across the railroad tracks about half a football field up the river. Let's go. Billy Bob led him to a muddy section of bank where some brush grew. Is this where they were found, Billy Bob? Yep, right out there about 15 feet or so where it gets deeper. Mary and Rigoberto were also tied up with boat rope. Billy Bob replied, What are the odds?

Billy Bob, I don't mind telling you I believe all these murders are connected and done by the same person. You can tell all that after being here just a couple hours? Believe it or not, Billy Bob, I've been studying this case for more than a day. We're going to catch this killer and lock him up for the rest of his life.

A web sleuth yells, Over here! Wienke and Billy Bob look over and the sleuth snaps their picture.

Chapter 7.

Dear Diary,

Scorpions can travel in pairs after all. They are also the protectors of evil, and they certainly did this time. Sometimes, I admire and even empathize with the victims, but ultimately we are all dead. They were rodents like that chinchilla that I crushed. I put them out of their miserable existence. They should've known to stay away.

Mary and Rigoberto crabbed and were insolent—I gave them a purpose. A different kind of purpose if you will, a King's gambit so to speak.

It's countdown to extinction for these pests. I'm more like a cockroach—I can survive nuclear fallout. But not them.

Billy Bob and his lovely wife Margarita were out with their friends Fernanda Escobedo de Diaz and Porfirio Diaz. They needed some time to unwind and have some fun. Fernanda is Margarita's friend from college. They both went to UTEP and obtained doctorate degrees in psychology. Fernanda is a forensic psychologist while Margarita went on to obtain her M.D. in psychiatry. Billy Bob considers himself lucky to get all the free therapy he could ask for—and more. Fernanda was a Mexican foreign exchange student.

Margarita has many friends and is well liked; Billy Bob not so much. People often wondered why they were together because of the glaring differences between them.

Porfirio wanted to go to the Sun Brewing Motel to have some beer and a bite to eat. Margarita was worried Billy Bob would be pulled into work, but Billy Bob couldn't help showing off his beer and cuisine. He reserved a table in the back patio in a somewhat secluded area where they could view the majestic borderland night. The light show over the Rio Grande and the mountains was something of profound beauty, the red western sky burning up as all the stars came out.

Billy Bob's unique personality is shining through as usual. He tells Porfirio while chuggling a beer, I'm a beer drinker, Porfirio. All these snob neophytes come here to taste beer and act like they know something when really it's all to impress somebody. It's more a facade than deep knowledge. I never just *taste* beer. I love it too much for that. What's even more baffling is how a BJCP judge cannot even judge a true wild sour ale or a 100% spontaneous ale properly. Goes to show you that even if you can regurgitate information and pass a test, doesn't mean you're really good.

Porfirio responds, I can see how that would agitate you. Firkin-A right, Porfirio. Some people shouldn't be judging beer at the highest levels; it's all status to them. Margarita tells them, Billy Bob is under a lot of stress lately with all the media and police attention this place has been getting. Fernanda nods. Yes, it must be a tremendous hardship, Billy Bob. Billy Bob replies, It is, but I'm glad I'm here with you lovely people drinking my own beer.

They all sip their beers, then he adds, I have a good olfactory. I can smell Fernanda's perfume. I have a nose like a bloodhound. Fernanda giggles with a bright smile. Billy Bob asks, What is that lovely aroma, Fernanda? Fernanda replies, That's Chanel number 5.

Billy Bob says, That is an apocryphal, ingenious, satisfying aroma around your neck. I think I'll make a beer with that aroma. It's floral with jasmine and rose, with a woody vanilla herbal undertone. Margarita pulls out her hot Cheetos and lights up a cigarette. Billy Bob quickly responds, Hot Cheetos and a cigarette? I can't believe you're lighting up. I expected the hot Cheetos, but the cigarette? You're really letting your hair down tonight, bonita. You typically only light up on special occasions. Margarita, just smiles and says, It's my guilty pleasure. Fernanda giggles. Margarita has always been her own person. I always love the crazy clothes she finds.

Billy Bob asks Maggie, Would you please put in for my sampler plate as an appetizer and for myself another Tamale Top Barleywine, thank you. Anything for you, Billy Bob! Billy Bob says, Gosh, I love Maggie. She's a hard worker and very proficient too. It's so hard to find good workers nowadays. I'll take someone with no skill and train them as long as they're a good worker with a good personality. I'll never work with a no-character person. I'll get rid of them. A lazy person will never amount to anything, no matter how talented. But a hard worker, I'll go to battle with on the front lines. Porfirio says, That's an interesting perspective. You seem to know people well. Thank you, Porfirio. You're going to love this sampler plate; it has my beer-bread pigs in a blanket, chamoy wings, stout beer-battered wings, with a bloomin' onion served with my beer boom boom sauce.

Porfirio says, This is a very interesting menu. I've never seen anything quite like it. You have so many beers that I've never heard of. Tepache Ale? Tamarindo Ale? It's hard to choose. You even have an Avocado Ale and a Mole Ale! What would you recommend? All of them Porfirio, but what kind of beer do you gravitate towards? Are you in the mood for a dark beer or a classic Mexican lager? Do you want it high ABV to knock you off your feet or do you want something that is low ABV that is lighter in taste and easy gulping? I have a new beer out called Rio de Piedad Lager which is a malty, dark, medium-bodied beer that finishes dry. If you feel experimental let me know, too, because I have a beer made with smoked pig heads in it, it's a porter from my Lunatic series of beers.

Fernanda smiles and says I'll pass on the pig head beer, but thank you. What kind of beer is Rio de Piedad Billy Bob? Rio de Piedad is an unfiltered Mexican style Vienna lager. It's made with water straight from the Rio Grande. I think the water from the Rio Grande gives the beer a spiritualness to it. Fernanda's eyes light up and she rubs her leg on Billy Bob's discreetly and tells him, surprise me Billy Bob; you pick for me. Billy Bob acts like nothing happened and hopes Porfirio and Margarita didn't notice and get the wrong idea. Perhaps Fernanda made a mistake, or perhaps it wasn't as sexy as he thought and she just accidentally brushed against him. Except it seemed extremely deliberate and rather sensual. Billy Bob calls for Maggie, Would you please get my good friend Porfirio here the Arkhangelisk RIS, and a Rio de Piedad for Fernanda here. What's that Billy Bob? A RIS is a Russian Imperial Stout. It's a dark beer, usually black; mine is black with ruby red hues. The flavor is deep and complex. The aroma is of rich dark fruity esters. You'll get bready, roasty dark cocoa, and plum, and it has a velvety, luscious, full-bodied mouthfeel.

Fernanda jokes, I do like a luscious mouthfeel, and everyone chuckles, but the toe of her she runs up Billy Bob's calf. Billy Bob says to her, It'll put hair on your chest, anyway. Porfirio and me will be howling at the moon tonight. Ah-ooooooooo, Aoo-Aoo, Ah-oooooo... Margarita says to Fernanda, Billy Bob is howling again.

Fernanda says, What would recommend to eat, Billy Bob? You even have chapulines! That's right. If you want tacos, you can't go wrong with chapulines or the fish, but if you want taquitos then I would go with the meatloaf or the corn beef flautas. Fernanda says, You know, Billy Bob, underneath that hillbilly accent and exterior of yours, you're really Mexican. Well, I try Fernanda. Thank you. Billy Bob tells Porfirio, Because you're drinking a RIS, you're going to want something very hearty and not too spicy. You might want to try my Beer-Nuts Pork Chops or the prime rib. The Billy Bob Steak isn't bad, either, but if you want something lighter, then the Beer-Battered Frog Legs are one of my of favorites. If you eat the prime rib or Billy Bob Steak, you're done for the night buddy.

Billy Bob asks Maggie, Would you be so kind as to bring Fernanda another Nincompoop IPA, and for my darling Margarita, here, please bring another Invictus. She loves my 100% spontaneous ales. Actually Maggie, bring her a Sun Equinox, that's my latest 100% spontaneous ale. Oh, and please put some Ozzy on, "Bark at the Moon." I know I'm a tough customer, Maggie, but thank you very much. Margarita says, Billy Bob, I can't believe you still listen to Ozzy and Iron Maiden. Yep. Ever since I was a tween, thank you very much.

Margarita, what are you going to order, my sugar-boo? I'll have the mole short ribs. No, this time I'll go with the chicken pipián. Let me guess what you're going to order, she says to her husband. Am I so predictable? he says. Yes, she says and blows him a kiss. You're going to have Granny's Fried Chicken or the Burrito de Pendejo. Billy Bob says, Close, but nope. I love Granny's Fried Chicken, but I love my Hot Fried Chicken even more. Billy Bob looks up at the sky and says, Sorry, Granny. I love the chili heat.

Margarita looks a little put out by this surprise. She'd hoped to show off how well she and Billy Bob vibe, but instead he's showing off all on his own. Fernanda looks down and tries to hide a snicker, but she can tell Margarita noticed. Burrito de Pendejo? says Fernanda. Idiot's Burrito? What a funny name. Don't people take offence to that kind of thing? Billy Bob replies, I've never cared what people think, then he looks up into the sky and says, Except my dear grandma. Anyway, you don't do the things that I do if you're always thinking about how you'll be received. Porfirio said, Isn't that a bit risky, considering you're in the service industry? Billy Bob replied, Yep, I've had a lot of people tell me that, but I yams what I yams—just like Popeye. I can't change that.

Fernanda, the Burrito de Pendejo was my grandma's concoction. It's a nice, quick burrito for the family made with simple items from the fridge. I always loved the pendejo, it's comforting. I was going to order a Rodeo Clown Burger or my Hot Fried Chicken Sandwich, but you know what I'm going to go with? Our Stout Beer Goat Stew with my Pale Ale Pretzels. I love to dip the pretzels into the stew. I'll also get some tostadas with salsa. We use hatch green chilis in our green salsa and make it real gourmet style. Margarita says, He thinks everything is gourmet down to the grilled cheese. My grilled cheese *is* real gourmet stuff, the way I make it! Porfirio says, You two make a great couple. Fernanda adds, Billy Bob is a funny guy. All women like a man with a sense of humor. Margarita tries to hide a frown and says, Being married to Billy Bob is one hell of a roller coaster ride. Then Billy Bob says, My smoochie-poo is what keeps us together, ladies and gentlemen.

Billy Bob asks Fernanda, What are your hobbies nowadays? Actually, I've been taking flamenco lessons. Wow, that's impressive. Billy Bob unconsciously looks her up and down as he says, I bet you dance real good. Margarita pinches him under the table. Ow, I mean, uh, I wish I could dance... Well, technically, I do dance a lot. I'm not shy, but I look like a dodo bird when I do. It's all good. I remember this one time I was dancing in the middle of the floor like in the Bangles song "Walk Like an Egyptian," and I knocked into a table and spilled beer all over my pants. Margarita thought I had pissed myself. Fernanda and Porfirio laugh and Fernanda slaps the table. Margarita and Fernanda exchange looks and giggle.

Then Margarita says Fernanda is working on a book on forensic psychology using the murders at the Sun Brewing Motel as a case study. Billy Bob doesn't look so happy about this, but he burst out, I've been writing a lot, too, lately. You want to hear my poem that I just wrote? Fernanda responds, Sure, we'd love to.

> Little yellow birdie lands upon my window sill
> It woke me up then I smashed his head
> Upon my window sill.

Margarita grimaces and says, That's it? There's more, baby doll. Margarita says, Oh, well, we can't wait to hear it. You're right, never mind on that one. I have one for you, Margarita. I just wrote this one, too:

> Roses are Red
> Violets are Blue
> Let's get naked
> And do what we do

What do you think, my sugar-boo? Let's play big chief, too. Margarita turns to their friends. That's not the booze talking, that's Billy Bob's everyday winning personality. Billy Bob says, Do you think I'm a creative genius, bonita? You did create Frankenstein barbecue sauce. That alone should seal the deal on your creative genius abilities. Billy Bob replies, I love it when I make an ingenious sauce. To hear the burbling in the saucepan. And I love you, bonita. You know where I have to take you guys next, Porfirio? Where's that? The Kentucky Club across the border in Juarez. It's the birthplace of the margarita and I took my lovely wife Margarita over there for a margarita. It was perfect. The Kentucky Club is world famous. I think even John Wayne had one there. Movie stars, politicians, and poets like me all come there to drink and rub elbows.

Margarita says, Those were the good ole days before we had a business to run. We had a lot of good times together, Guapo.

Porfirio says to Billy Bob, I have a question for you: How did all these places like your Sun Brewing Motel and The Kentucky Club survive the pandemic? Good question. Sometimes it takes a little luck. We're all coming close to extinction unless you're big business. Everything's all changed. No more dive bars, which I used to truly love, myself. The dive was once a humble and sacred establishment for an eclectic group of locals. Every generation from Generation X and earlier grew up with a dive establishment. Nowadays, businesses are redefining everything from fancy affairs to casual environment. Small business isn't small business anymore. A lot of them are million-dollar businesses out the gate. If there were any true mom and pop's out there, then the odds are they're going under unless they're some kind of legacy where they own their own land already. The only ones who could really survive are the big money establishments. They can wait it out with their deep pockets. Me personally, I'll do anything to save my business and keep my dream alive. That will also take changing the hearts and minds of the masses of people, because countless studies show people are increasingly gravitating towards big businesses. Times have changed and people's values have changed. Porfirio sighs with compassion. I can see your passion, Billy Bob. Do you think it'll circle back and level itself out? It looks doubtful. There isn't much substance anymore. There's a lot of clamor for cheap status and to look good. Porfirio says, Yes, but will small businesses make a comeback from the pandemic? Unfortunately, a lot of them won't. Some will, of course—especially the ones who distribute. The big-enough businesses who can distribute can minimize loss and re-invent themselves a teensy bit to focus on their core lineup. The true small businesses are in a lot of trouble, though. A lot of them took government money to stay afloat. I never took government money for help because I knew there would be a day Uncle Sam would come a knocking for his money back. I never trusted it. So, I did whatever it took to stay afloat. I could write a thousand-page book on it because it was a lot.

Can you give us the bird's-eye view? It must have been difficult to survive. It was. First, I offered my COVID emergency packs when it looked like the world had gone mad. You couldn't find toilet paper anywhere and people were really panicking. It was a real mess. I used my connections to get a generous order of toilet paper, and I was out there in the streets with a sign that read: COVID Emergency Packs – Get your 6-pack of beer, two rolls of toilet paper, and taco 12-packs. It was pure madness, but them COVID emergency packs really paid dividends. It allowed me to shift gears to beer and food to go. It also allowed me to streamline my menu to the bare essentials. There are a lot of menu items that you don't really make money off of, so we cut them and only focused on the tried-and-true items. It takes a little luck also, because of all of the uncertainty to everything. I wouldn't blame anyone for closing down for a couple of years just to resurface when the time is right, but who really knows how this is going to end up? We are still in the aftermath of the main COVID variants and there is no clear path going forward. The way the world does business very well may be changed forever.

Billy Bob sees Maggie with a huge tray and cries, The food is here! It's time to dig in. Bon appetit! The hungry friends dive into their dinners. I should have ordered the hueraches or discada tacos, Billy Bob says. This goat stew is heavy and makes me want to just sit here and not get up. How's your prime rib, Porfirio? Excellent, thank you. You know, I've noticed a lot of Mexican's eat their steak well done. Me, I love mine bloody as hell. Yes, it's true, we Mexicans don't like any food bloody. How's them fish tacos, Fernanda? They're fabulous, Billy Bob. Margarita says the chicken pipián is okay. Billy Bob comments, Margarita is hard to please. She sticks her tongue out at him, but Fernanda thinks it's not entirely in jest.

Billy Bob tells Porfirio, I got a gift for you and Fernanda. He signals to Chino, who comes over with two large bottles of beer. It's one bottle each from my Trivium series of 100% spontaneous ales. Each bottle is 750 mL, aged five years, and clocking in at 9.2% ABV. You can't find anything in the world like it. It's unique to this area because of the wild yeasts. Wow, Billy Bob, this is amazing Fernanda replies and Porfirio says, Thank you very much, my friend. Billy Bob says, It's the terroir, the environment, that makes these beers special because they can never be duplicated. They're unique to this region. Porfirio responds, Like, indigenous. Yep, that's correct; it's an indigenous beer. Thank you very much, Billy Bob. You're welcome, and I hope you enjoy it.

Billy Bob looks down toward the river. Hey, he says, the night is young and there's a full moon out. Let's take some beer and jump into the Rio. Porfirio cheers, Yes, a walk along the river would be lovely. Margarita says, No, Billy Bob is being serious. He's always been attracted to the Rio Grande for some reason. Billy Bob, you can jump into the Rio Grande and we'll watch. Vamos canijotes! Let's go, Porfirio! Thanks, but I think I'll stay with my wife. But Fernanda says, No, let's go to the river. Billy Bob cries, I guess it's settled! I'll grab the brewskis.

Margarita goes with her husband. Please behave yourself down there. Don't embarrass me. Of course, bonita. I probably won't jump in the rio or start howling at the moon until everyone is happy enough not to remember anything anyway. They rejoin the others and he cracks open a Czech pilsner while they walk down to the rio. He starts telling them ghost stories about the Rio Grande.

Porfirio says, Maybe ghosts are murdering your guests. That would be one explanation, says Margarita. Fernanda rolls her eyes at Porfirio, then from behind her Billy Bob shouts, Boo! Fernanda nearly jumped out of her dress and shrieked. She turned around and slapped Billy Bob on the arm. Don't *do* that!

Fernanda is getting a little scared, the Rio Grande at night is secluded and dark. You can hear the slightest of sounds as you walk down the rio at night. Billy Bob tells them, You know voices are often heard while walking down the rio. Legend has it that lost souls dwell in the river at night and you can sometimes see hands clawing out of the river banks. Margarita says, That's enough. Fernanda spooks easy. Or am I spooking you, bonita? Aye, you believe in La Llorona. Maybe we'll hear her tonight!

Fernanda says her nanny used to terrify her with stories of La Llorona. Billy Bob has taken off his shoes and socks. He runs into the water and says, I should write a folk song about La Llorona. Something like...

> La la... la la la la... la la Llorona
> La la... la la Llorona and the Boogyman
> La la... la la Llorona and the Boogyman drink black and tan's
> La la Llorona
> La la Llorona
> La la... la la Llorona is a chichona and loves Corona
> La la Llorona
> La la Llorona
> La la... la la Llorona and the Cucuy
> La la... la la Llorona and the Cucuy do Kung Fuey while eating Chop Suey
> La la... la la la la... la la Llorona

Come on in, the water's great! Margarita rolls her eyes and walks down the shore. Porfirio follows her. Fernanda giggles but kicks off her shoes and walks into the water. Billy Bob kicks water at her; she responds in kind, and soon they're soaked and laughing.

Porfirio had thought his wife was behind him, so he's surprised to turn and see her way back with Billy Bob in the water. Margarita says, They're getting chummy. She's had a lot to drink, says Porfirio. Billy Bob, too, Margarita agrees. Maybe we should head back before somebody does something stupid.

Hey, kids, let's head back, Porfirio calls when they draw near. Yeah, alright, says Billy Bob. He and Fernanda come out of the water and sit in the grass. Everyone takes a breather and enjoys the cool night air. Then Porfirio says, Do you hear that? Billy Bob says, Hear what? Someone is over there across the river, in that bush. Billy Bob replies, What, in that big shrubbery? Probably a squirrel or coyote. I love Texas shrubberies. Fernanda says, Let's head back and call it a night. Margarita gasps. I think I saw a person. Someone's watching us from the other side. Billy Bob said, Don't worry, baby doll. They can't do us any harm from over there. Anyway, I got my pistola and it barks loud and bites far away. Billy Bob tells Porfirio and Fernanda, I got the El Presidente room ready for you if you want to stay the night. Fernanda replies, I would love that. Let's stay the night, Porfirio.

Billy Bob takes them to the El Presidente room and shows them how much he loves this room. He said, I designed this room myself. That's a whiskey barrel for beer baths, if you'd like to partake, and this is a special wrought-iron spiral staircase to the top of the motel for your own stargazing and uranology. You got your own bar here and vibrating massager, too. I love to put that thing on my neck. Porfirio says, This room feels like I've gone back in time to the 70s. Billy Bob responds, Exactly! I love the 70s. I love the design and fashion. Things seemed so much simpler than today. I used a pay phone if I needed to call someone, and now I have to watch my wife glued to her smart phone every time we go out. I used to have dozens of phone numbers by memory. I also would have actually wanted to talk if I called someone. Fernanda says, That's true. Maybe we'll pretend it's 1974 while we're here. Billy Bob adds, You know what else was great about the 70s? What, Billy Bob? The grand and superior style of it all... from the exquisite suits to the muscle cars. Nothing better than driving a 70s muscle car in a 70s suit. Now that's style. That's when Pontiac ruled them all. At any rate, have a good night, Porfirio, Fernanda. Enjoy.

Billy Bob goes back to Margarita's car and gets in. Okay, darlin', they are all set. Let's roll. It's starting to rain. Let's get to the casa. Margarita pulls out and they hit the road as scattered raindrops hit the windshield. When they arrive home, Margarita asks, Did you have a nice time with Fernanda? Billy Bob recalls the footplay under the table and immediately feels guilty. He says, Oh, I was just trying to be sociable. You were drunk, is what you were. Aw, honey bear, don't be like that. Hey, can I have a therapy session when we get home, darling? Not a good idea, Billy Bob. Maybe tomorrow morning if you're real nice to me. Oh, come on Margarita, just a little therapy, please. I love laying on the sofa while staring at the ceiling and talking randomly while drinking a beer. Okay, Billy Bob, but let's make it quick. You like to talk for hours and then you want me to tell you a bedtime story. Please tell me a bedtime story tonight, bonita! There will be no need, Billy Bob. You're going to end up passing out and snoring on the couch again. Okay, fine. I'll be waiting on my sofa. Billy Bob, if you're not passed out snoring, then you're waking up with nightmares. I'll be there in a minute.

Billy Bob lies on the sofa by his dog, Wolfie, and waits impatiently. Margarita shows up and sits at her desk. Billy Bob asks Margarita, Aren't you going to smile at me, darling? Margarita smiles and says, Aren't you going to ask me how Wolfie is doing? You're right: How is Wolfie? I imagine Wolfie is desperate for your attention, Billy Bob, because you're always working. Ah, yes, that's right, you were telling me in our last session about work/life balance. Let me ask you a question, Margarita: Were you really scared tonight? Yes, I was Billy Bob. I was also scared that you had a gun. You know Margarita, I carry that for protection, it's the wild, wild west out here. Billy Bob, you put yourself in risky situations that the average person wouldn't do. Why do you continue to do that? Like what, bonita? You go drinking in Juarez in the most dangerous of colonias while bar hopping to who knows where. You forget, Margarita, when I got out of the Marines, I lived in Juarez, Mexico. I know that city like the back of my hand. You don't see it, do you, Billy Bob? See what? Never mind. I have another question for you, Margarita: What did it feel like hearing about ghost stories while walking down the Rio Grande? It was creepy and uncomfortable, and all the while you were laughing it up, like it was extremely entertaining to you. Did you at least like my La Llorona song? ...and did you write it down? You're always super fanatical about writing all our sessions down and taking notes on me while we are out. Margarita laughs a little, I did jot it down, actually. Even your juvenile poem. Billy Bob replies, Go ahead and yuck it up... yuck, yuck, yuck. You know, Billy Bob, sometimes I wonder how I ever got involved with a guy like you. It's because of my Woody Woodpecker darling, Heh-heh-heh-Hehhh-heh. Margarita rolls her eyes. Why don't you go refresh that red lipstick of yours and make your hair floofy and get in that lingerie that I like, then come back and give Big Papi a smoochie-poo. Margarita leaves for several minutes.

When she comes back, Billy Bob is passed out and snoring loudly on the sofa. She returns to the bedroom.

At 11 a.m. the next morning, his phone starts ringing. Billy Bob is passed out on the couch and he doesn't even wake up the first three times and it goes to voicemail. The fourth and fifth times he rejects the call because he wants to brush his teeth and take a Tylenol. He has voicemail notifications and texts galore. Billy Bob finally answers the phone. It's. Peter.

Billy Bob, where have you been? Porfirio's here and he's freaking out. Fernanda has gone missing!

Chapter 8.

Dear Diary,

Sorrow at the Sun Frills Motel and that which is not sorrow not blinded by the light.

Sometimes sorrow follows me, like Pig-Pen's cloud—but not today.

I'm standing in acid rain as the death bell rings.

They avoid the light—whoever has love also has pain and sorrow.

I won't stop loving you, but nothing will stop my reign.

The beautiful attire you wore.

I see you, Madonna-whore.

Nobody knows what's in my head until I write and even then I'm not sure it's conveyed right. Nobody knows what's in my heart unless I write and even then am I only seeing in black and white?

I write and I write even in Crayola and it's a window into my soul for Diary.

I've always loved Diary;

Diary really gets me.

I remember first thinking about Diary as a child... Oh, wow, Diary really gets me. I was in them special classes for the troubled. It was the start of a beautiful relationship. Maybe Diary is cryptic at times or conveying another direct compulsion.

I look back to when my joker syndrome first caught people's attention when I was an adolescent and that's when I realized I can get out of this depression. It's also when I realized I don't always have to laugh out loud, it is controllable to a certain degree. I can kind of sneeze-laugh or hurt myself.

I'm happy. I'm sad. I'm depressed.

All the birds have flown for Fernanda.

Billy Bob calls Lt. Wienke and informs him of the situation. This isn't good, sir. I'm worried something might happen to her. Mr. Wienke says, Call the police and get them on the scene right away, then meet me at the motel. What he doesn't say is that, if this disappearance follows the others, whatever might happen to Fernanda has already happened.

Wienke and Coffee arrive at the motel at the same time as Det. Martinez, Dep. Martinez, and a forensics crew. It's clear they're treating this like a crime scene. Porfirio is a blubbering mess. Peter sticks him in Billy Bob's office to calm down. After a moment of consultation, the cops start to search Fernanda's room and the general motel premises. Wienke's team begins to record interviews with everyone and take their own pictures and look about.

Late in the day, everyone's story matches up so far. Porfirio was the last person to see her. She stepped out to get ice and never returned. He had passed out on the bed and didn't notice until morning. No one had seen her in the restaurant, on the patio, by the river, or anywhere.

Margarita is taking it hard that her friend Fernanda is missing and is going through a depression. Margarita bakes a lot when she is depressed, and for the next several days she brings out her fresh-baked cookies to Billy Bob on their back patio at home. Billy Bob starts to worry about her, so on the fourth day, when she comes out with another plate of cookies, he jumps up and begins to clown around.

Oh... My... Gosh! COOOOOOOKIES! Well stand up and slap Grandma! He stuffs a whole cookie in his mouth and lets the crumbs fall like Cookie Monster. These cookies are simply delicious, bonita, he says with his mouth still half full. My favorite: chocolate chip. Just like Grandma used to make. Billy Bob looks up to the sky and starts talking to Grandma again. Grandma, your legacy lives on in my lovely wife, Margarita! She has mastered the lessons you taught her and is making your grandson a very happy boy. Margarita at last cracks a smile, shaking her head in embarrassment.

I have a serious question for you, bonita. What's that? Doesn't the moon look like a giant coooookie? Margarita rolls her eyes, but now she's full-on smiling. She says, Pancita llena, corazón contento. (full belly, happy heart). Margarita tells Billy Bob, I'm going to San Eli tomorrow. I'll be back soon. I know, bonita. You keep coming back. But what is it? Is it my fortune or my fame? It's because of your winning personality Billy Bob. You're charming and sooo romantic. Okay, darling, be safe, and please bring me back some of them San Eli tortillas. They're my favorite—outside of yours, of course.

Billy Bob is acting casual, but he knows this isn't good. Whenever Margarita gets really upset, she takes off to San Elizario, where she is originally from. She'll go to the Three Missions from the borderlands. Billy Bob and Margarita were married in the San Eli Presidio chapel. The original chapel was a Spanish military chapel built in the 1500s. It was burned down when it was the country of Nueva España (New Spain). After the Mexican revolution, a new country was forming in the early to middle 1800s named after the capital city of New Spain, called Los Estados Unidos de México. The chapel was rebuilt in 1877 as a Mexican replica of the original

Spanish colonial style chapel. The San Eli Presidio isn't really a mission like the Socorro and Ysleta missions are, but because of its history they call it The Three Missions Trail for tourists to visit. Tourists love to visit where Billy the Kid was captured in San Eli and where he was put in the San Elizario jail. Margarita takes comfort in going there; it levels her out. She'll come home with some candles from the missions and light them as prayers.

A couple more days pass and Lt. Wienke pays Billy Bob a visit at the motel. He wants to go over the official statements again and go back to the room Fernanda and Porfirio were staying in. Wienke isn't giving out many new details of the case to Billy Bob— or to Porfirio, who has been spending his days going back and forth from his home to the motel. Just that morning Wienke had executed a search warrant for Porfirio and Fernanda's house. I can assure you, Mr. Diaz, we are going to find out who, how, and why this happened. We are in the process of getting phone records, and we also found Fernanda's diary. Did you know your wife believed you were having an affair? Me? Why? I mean, no, I had no clue.What did she say? Billy Bob shakes his head, This is like I thought all along. People are coming to the Sun Brewing Motel to commit crimes against humanity.

Now a pickup truck reading Policía Federal pulls up. Billy Bob notices out the window and says, Hey, now, you didn't tell us Mexico was getting involved. What else aren't you telling us?

A short but serious-looking German-Mexican man steps out of the car. He has bleach-blonde hair with crystal blue eyes and is dressed very old-fashioned with grey Wrangler rancher dress slacks and classic Mexican cowboy boots with white button-up shirt and sport jacket. Peter greets him at the door, then escorts him over to Billy Bob, Porfirio, and Wienke and makes introductions. This is the owner, Billy Bob. This is Porfirio Diaz. And this is Texas Ranger

Wienke. Gentlemen, this is Egon Krahn of the Mexican Federal Police. He's here to help with the investigation into the death of Fernanda Diaz.

Death? says Porfirio. No... He steps off his barstool and crumples onto the floor, holding the back of a nearby chair for support.

Wienke, what's this about? says Billy Bob. I didn't mean to tell you quite yet, but Mexican authorities found Fernanda Diaz's body near the Rio Grande—on the Mexican side of the river—late last night. The Texas Rangers will be coordinating with the Mexican authorities on the investigation. Mrs. Diaz's body will remain in Mexico for the time being. Now, can we get some coffees while we discuss some particulars? Of course!

Peter helps Porfirio back to Billy Bob's office. Egon Krahn and John John Coffee sit at a table while Wienke steps outside to take a call. Billy Bob sits at the bar and calls to Krahn, Hey, do you know how she died? Krahn says, We're not prepared to say at this time, I'm afraid. Chino comes out with coffees and asks Krahn where in Mexico he's from. Krahn says, I'm from Mazatlán, and my father and my father's father and their fathers are, too. Chino looks at Krahn's blond hair and blue eyes and thinks he protests a bit too much about his Mexican credentials, but he says, I've heard great things about the great city of Mazatlán. I've always wanted to take a vacation there and see all the culture.

Billy Bob is still at the bar but has overheard them. I've always wanted to go, too. I was close to going when I was in Durango to see an old friend get married but ended up staying in Durango for a while. Egon leans back like he's enjoying the casual conversation and says, Where else have you been in México, Billy Bob? Oh, here and there. When I was a lot younger, I got in my Volkswagen Beetle with some friends and drove down Baja, California, stopped in Tijuana, then made my way to Rosarito Beach where I passed out in the sand with a bottle of mezcal. Then we finally made our way to Ensenada. We packed hippie food for the trip and ended up eating burritos in every single pueblo we came across. We got lost on our way back and wound up going through the city of Tecate. Yeah, I drank some Tecates there, my friend. Egon smiles and says, Had a good time, did you? ¡Si, claro! You see, my cousin Joe was smoking a joint in the back seat while me and my buddy Raul were up front, and the second-hand smoke got us all high. I was driving about 5 miles an hour and wondering why everyone was passing us. Some grandma even passed by and flipped us off. Raul was confused too and kept asking, Why are going only 5 miles per hour? Only, I thought he was exaggerating. It turned out we had two flat tires. So, we stopped to get them fixed and had some burritos and Tecates while we waited. I want to be clear, though, that I'm not a doper. I don't do drugs. It's just that the second-hand smoke really did a number on us all. Some kid had come up to us in Tijuana and asked us if we wanted some wacky weed. I thought nothing of it, but Joe bought some grass from the kid and we didn't even know about it. He's always wandering off doing his own thing. Joe is a real hippie, you know?

Egon is still smiling. You have a lot to say, amigo. We should go out for a beer sometime and share stories. Heck, yeah! Come by some time and I'll make you my famous chimichanga. It goes down real good with a lager. Egon replies, Thank you Billy Bob. I've heard you're a great brewer and chef. But I know that you've lived in México before. You lived in Juarez from September 2007 to August 2009. That sounds right. What made you live there, Billy Bob? That's a long story, but I'll try to sum it up.

Okay, so I had just gotten out of the Marines after all them combat tours in Iraq and Afghanistan. I saw some messed up stuff, and I needed somewhere to go and make a new start. My old friend from childhood, Raul, who I went to elementary, middle, and high school with, had moved to Juarez because he married a Mexican señorita from Durango. His plan was to live in Juarez until he could get stuff straightened out with her family and bring them all over to El Paso. He had a very nice house in Colonia Casas Grandes. It didn't look like much from the outside, just a regular home, but on the inside, it had everything: upstairs swimming pool and grill, downstairs recreation room, and a lot more. So, he had plenty of room for me, and he invited me to live with him because I've always loved it there. I took him up on his offer and lived with him and his family until I could branch out on my own.

Egon said, Two years is a long time. Billy Bob said, Yeah, but they were the kindest people. I ended up wanting to buy his house and stay, but we all had a change of plans and moved back to El Paso. Egon said, You mean you moved back because of the violence. Billy Bob replied, Yeah, it was sad, but it was a long time coming if you ask me. Things happened kinda slowly in Juarez, so I didn't realize it until I lived there for a while. What did you realize, Billy Bob? Well, I'm from the borderlands and I know that Coronado High School had its own bar in J-Town called Superior. That's comical because they were considered the snob school of El Paso. Juarez was truly an international city with millions of people and it was safe for the most part. You would see Americans with their entire families walking across the border going to the mercados, eating, listening to music or catching a movie, and shopping. Movie stars, politicians, and other influential people would visit world-famous bars like the Kentucky Club—which I'm sure you know is the birthplace of the margarita. I loved going to the Nebraska bar when I was a young teen. If you weren't looking for trouble, then you were okay, nobody would mess with you. The military from Fort Bliss would hang out at Spanky's, a Rock 'N' Roll bar. They'd get into brawls all the time, but you lived another day and there was no vendetta. It was a total win-win for everyone, a cultural exchange that allowed us to enrich each other in many ways. Today, sadly it's a ghost town for businesses and everyone is afraid because of random violence. Businesses being burned down and people kidnapped.

Why do you think everything changed, Billy Bob? I think Pre-9/11, everyone was profiting, but Post-9/11 you seen the entire world change, especially with border security and border business. 9/11 caused a slow change not only in the entire world but especially in Juarez because there wasn't enough flourishing businesses and jobs, which meant the prime industry of tourism completely stopped. The piece of the pie got smaller for everyone, and everyone was fighting over it. There is a little more to it than that but that's the gist of it. I'm not saying I really know, but that's what I think and what I believe for what and why it happened.

Egon said, Juarez, for that time period that you lived there, was one of the most dangerous cities in the entire world, and you were living there going to bars and eating burritos and dreaming of buying property. It was probably as dangerous as some of them places you've been to in the Middle East. That's true, it was, but in the Middle East an American wouldn't last a day without being abducted, I was in the Marines. The violence in Juarez is different. If you know how to conduct yourself in Juarez and stay clean by not looking for trouble, then you should be okay. I remember it was hard to tell the difference in Juarez between the military and the gangsters. When I would go home to Colonia Casas Grandes there would be check points with people in blue cargo pants, black sweaters, and ski masks with machine guns stopping to check me. They would talk to me in Spanish, asking me questions... I would respond (I can habla some Español), I told them: Amigos, amigos tengo amor por Juárez y quiero señoritas and margaritas! I always survived; my wife says it's my winning personality. Most people think I'm crazy for living in Juarez during that time frame, but that's essentially the reasons I moved to Juarez. Egon just smiles at Billy Bob and nods.

Wienke returns and says, That man will talk the ears off an elephant if you let him. Egon says, Quite alright. I appreciate the hospitality and conversation. I came to get to know the people at this poor motel, after all. You folks have been through a lot in the last couple years. I'd like to meet and talk to everyone. I'd also like to look at the motel room Fernanda was in.

Billy Bob takes Egon and the others down to the room. Bianca, the cleaning lady, is a couple doors down, but Krahn asks to speak to her. You discovered Ms. Daisy Swallows' absence, isn't that right? Si, señor. And I understand that was a distressing and, shall we say, surprising sight. Si, si. Did you notice anything going on in el Presidente room before or after Mrs. Diaz went missing? Bianca hesitates, but says no.

Egon asks Bianca, You know, I'm getting hungry. What do you say I take you for a quick lunch? Bianca looks at Billy Bob, who says, Go ahead, Bianca. We want to cooperate with these gentlemen. Anywhere we can get good Mexican food around here? Billy Bob interrupts, Sr. Krahn, you're in El Paso. We have great Tex-Mex, Borderlands cuisine, so much to offer. I'm not here as a tourist, Billy Bob. Bianca says, People like Elemi's for fine dining Mexican food, Lupita's for tamales and pigs feet, and The Little Diner for gorditas. Where would you like to go Bianca? Me personally, I like Lucy's because it's a real small café with not too many people where I can have something simple like huevos rancheros and a coffee. Egon says, Let's go for good coffee and huevos rancheros.

Egon sits and talks with Bianca and gets to know her and even starts to like her. She told him about her Tourette's and how she learned to live with it. I've been going to church more, now that I'm not always disrupting the service. I light a candle every time. I love the Saint Jude candle. I have one at home that I light for the Sun Brewing Motel. What's Saint Jude's specialty, again? Desperate or...hopeless causes. You think it's that bad? For the families, I expect. I agree with you there.

Look, Bianca, the real reason I brought you here is I suspect you've been wanting to say something that you don't think you should say, or perhaps that you think we won't believe. Do you know something about Fernanda, Daisy, or Isabella? Do you have a theory about why they went missing? She replied, I don't know how to say. You are a good man, Sr. Krahn. You must not make a fool of me. Of course not, Bianca. Tell me. Sometimes...I hear things. I think I hear things. In the walls. Like someone walking. Someone walking? Like, a woman or a man? Clip-clop, like high heels, only quiet. Is there a service passage behind the rooms? Not that I know of. So what do you think it is?

Bianca leans in and whispers, I think I hear that sound another time. It is the ghost of Isabella Mata!

Egon can feel he's on the verge of something important. Tell me more, he says. The day I find Isabella Mata's room all a mess, I hear the clip-clop sound. It sounds like it comes from behind the cuckoo clock. The cuckoo clock? Sí. The rooms are very old-fashioned. They all have cuckoo clocks on their back walls. Show me.

They return to the motel and Bianca takes him to an empty room. Peter notices them pull up and grabs Billy Bob, and they all go in together. Egon scrutinizes the cuckoo clock. This is pretty fancy, Billy Bob, he says. You buy these for all the rooms? No, sir. I love them cuckoo clocks though. They came with the rooms, and I liked the idea to decorate them.

Egon pulls a chair under the clock and stands on it. He tries to remove the clock from the wall, but it is bolted on rather tight and he can't budge it. He flips open the cuckoo's door and pushes and pulls at other parts of the clock face, then sighs in frustration. What is it? Billy Bob asks. That's just the problem, says Egon. It looks like nothing...

Chapter 9.

Dear Diary,

I just took my meds and I'm waiting to feel good. Never seems to work.

It's time to howl at the moon and write a poem today called Little Red Fernanda.

Or maybe I'll call it Little Red Fernanda Walking Down the Ol' Spooky River Alone.

I'll stick to the original metaphors and keep it Little Red Riding Hood. A lot can be learned from the Little Red Riding Hood fairy tale. Little Red Riding Hood represents the Sun and righteousness. The big, bad wolf represents the dark and what's rotten at its core even though the wolf seems harmless at first. It's the cycle of life and the wolf wants to swallow the sun. The ones who seem harmless are the ones to fear the most.

Awoooooh!

That's Little Red Riding Hood.

You sure are smelling good.

I see you got goodies and a bottle of beer.

That red velvet is some fine warm gear.

Awooooh!

Whatcha doin' walkin' down this river alone?

Why, Little Red Riding Hood, aren't you afraid of the unknown?

You got to get to Grandma's place.
No worries, walk with me and be safe.
Awooooh!
Why, Little Red Riding Hood, what big eyes you have.
The softest eyes with no disguise.
What a beautiful smile you have.
The kind of smile that drives killers mad.
Awooooh!
Little Red Riding Hood, look, there's some sunflowers.
Fetch them for Grandma's place, I think you should.
Little Red Riding Hood, what big hands I have.
The better to hold you with, if I could.
What a big nose I have.
The better to sniff your goodies with.
Awooooh!
Little Red Riding Hood, I won't be satisfied.
Until I walk by your side.
Maybe Grandma would embrace.
I'll keep a try'n even though ya'll think I'm a nutcase.
Awooooh!
Little Red Riding Hood.
Just remember big, bad wolves can be good.
I think a little, good girl should.

With all the craziness of the world, when it's a little dark and a little dank, it's the brew day that sets Billy Bob right. Thousands of pounds of grain thrown over his shoulder and everything prepped for brewing. Rumor has it Billy Bob sleeps with his yeast for good luck and for yeast acclimation. He is always checking on the proprietary yeast strain for pitching. The fermentation part of brewing is what Billy Bob calls the truly divine part of it all, to see all the bubblies, the evidence of heavenly favor at work. Where would the world be without beer? Ask some of the first explorers from the Old World that traveled across the Atlantic using it for the basic ingredients for life on a long journey, like the Pilgrims or the ancient Egyptians who used it for currency, or how Europeans survived the black plague, or modern medicine, which would not exist if it wasn't for beer—antibodies were discovered from beer, after all. Billy Bob proudly tells his brewers about beer history all the time. Ah, yes, it's brew day, and it's time to make the world's greatest beverage that has all the essential nutrients, vitamins, and minerals to sustain life, not to mention the intangibles like pure joy.

It's brew day, and Billy Bob has designed a beer called Fernanda. It's an American lager brewed with adjuncts of flaked corn, roses, jasmine, and vanilla. People are already talking about the name of this beer. Some people are objecting to it while others are embracing it. Billy Bob says, It's an ode to our friend Fernanda, a liquid poem, but there's always going to be haters.

KVIA, the local ABC news station, is at the Sun Brewing Motel with legendary investigative reporters Iker Casillas and Elias Rockenstein. They're interviewing Peter while Chino "looks" for Billy Bob, who doesn't want to be disturbed on brew day. Web sleuths in Sun Brewing hats and T-shirts are milling about taking photos and video and recording themselves having nothing new to say other than there's rumors that Billy Bob is naming a beer after a murdered woman.

Then Egon Krahn pulls up. The web sleuths all gather at a short distance from him, sure he'll lead them to something interesting, while the KVIA team also gathers their gear and hustles over to attempt an interview. Chino had been watching from the kitchen, and now he runs to the brewery and says, Billy Bob, we got half of El Paso here looking to talk to you. Billy Bob runs to the kitchen and looks out the window. Wowza, this is too much heat for me, carnal. He runs out the back door, around the patio, and slips into his Volkswagen Beetle as quietly as he can, but when he starts it, everyone sees him and crowds around his car. Egon pushes his way through and knocks on the window. Mind if I ride along? Get me outta this craziness and I'll let you drink for free! Egon pulls out his badge and waves it around. I need everyone to take 10 paces backward right now! The crowd pouts but steps back, and Billy Bob and Egon drive off.

Billy Bob is going nowhere particular, just listening to music on a quiet road on the edge of town. He puts on Metallica's *And Justice for All*. Egon says, Wow, that's heavy. It's got to be to crowd out the rest of the noise. You know, Egon, the younger generation in Mexico love Metallica as much or more than the Americans—like the Mexicans are becoming more American than the Americans. Egon replies, That's crazy. Liking Metallica doesn't make you American. Billy Bob retorts, Just take a look at when Metallica plays at Azteca Stadium there in Mexico City. The stadium is packed to full capacity like a Mexico vs. USA soccer game, and even more people hang around the outside of stadium. The stadium is rocken like a low-grade earthquake. Egon says, That's just great, the degradation of our culture. Billy Bob switches the music to The Doors' *Roadhouse Blues*. Egon says, Where are we going, Billy Bob? Billy Bob responds, I'm on a highway to hell amigo. Let's go to J-Town. Lets go to Mexico and have some cervezas. Billy Bob and Egon cross the Puente Libre, a.k.a. the Free Bridge, and cross over to Juarez, Mexico. As they cross Billy Bob makes the sign of the cross like he was in Catholic mass. Egon says, Are you a religious man, Billy Bob? I was raised Roman Catholic because of my mom. She's a very old-fashioned chicana, very religious and spiritual.

They find a hole-in-the wall and sit down to drink cold Mexican beers. Billy Bob orders a shot of mezcal and Egon says, You really like mezcal, my friend. It's my favorite liquor, Egon. Anybody ever tell you you're reckless, Billy Bob? Yeah, only everybody I ever met. But there was once a time I was real sharp. I traveled the world making a difference when I was younger. Yes, I know. You were in the Marines. Billy Bob replies, Yes for the Marines, but I meant other jobs after that. You got around a bit, didn't you?

Billy Bob tells Egon, I'll share a story with you. Once I was in Russia, Moscow, and I'd walk the streets of Gorky Park and so on. We'd be going from bar to bar and we'd always see soldiers just out in the streets. You know, I looked at those Russian soldiers like brothers in arms. Like, we were technically not friends with them, but a man in uniform knows something about another man in uniform that you can't know if you've never worn that uniform. I have a great admiration for other militaries, especially the ones I've worked with like the Gurkhas and Korean ROC Marines. We military men are just that—not politicians or ideologues. We are on no one's side, red or blue. We simply do our job with honor. That's why, when I seen them walking by or when I was drinking beer in the bar having small talk, I realized our differences are really superficial. I really connected with them and loved the cultural exchange. I would love to make a good old-fashioned beef stroganoff, which I learned from an old guy in a bar. His grandma made it to perfection for him, growing up. I especially loved their Russian Kvas and tried to learn their cuisine. I ended up making my own beer based off of Russian Kvas. They were such a good and proud people doing the best they can with what they got. I distinctively remember thinking to myself, How can we be so alike and be considered enemies? I came to the conclusion that you can't judge a people by its government. I really loved Russia and the strong spirit of the people. When I looked at other countries I've been to and compared them to my own, I often wonder if America has lost its identity. Egon replies, Funny you should say that. I've felt the same about Mexico and America.

Egon tells Billy Bob a similar story from when he was in New York City on 9/11. I was walking through the famous Central Park when the twin towers came down. I remember seing first-hand the strength, resolve, and compassion of the American people. I distinctively remember thinking how the Americans and the Mexicans are really very similar and how you can't judge Americans by its government and leadership any more than you can Mexicans. The Mexican people are kind, giving, compassionate, and very strong.

Our countries are a lot alike. Both were based on being very conservative and religious and both are going through a transformation of greater liberalism. You spoke of America and its identity. It's the same in Mexico; we are figuring out our identity, too. Christopher Columbus statues are not just coming down in America—they're coming down in Mexico, too. Billy Bob replies, Christopher Columbus believed he would find Blemmyes and Sciapods in the new world. We're talking people with their faces in their chest or just one giant foot. In my view, it would be ridiculous to hold Columbus to the moral standards of today. He was several worlds away from us. How silly is it to hold someone from the 15th century to 21st century moral standards? I tell you Egon, I'd never put that on him or anyone from ancient history, just like I hope the future won't judge us too hard by their own standards.

I won't lose sleep over it either way, but my Italian friends? Every Italian I've ever known is proud of Christopher Columbus for being an Italian explorer to the new world. Egon says, It's what the educated elites call "decolonization." Billy Bob replies, That's a silly word if you ask me, Egon. I guess that's why I'm not an educated elitist. You can't decolonize; it's a silly concept. I think what you can do, Egon, is recognize everybody, Aztec and indigenous culture and the Spanish culture. You know Egon, Mexico wouldn't exist without all those influences. Mexico City was created as the capital of New Spain. There is a lot of other culture to recognize in Mexico from the Middle Eastern influences to the Asian immigrants' contributions and influences. German immigrants like your family, Egon. The Germans played a huge role in settling Mazatlán—and they brought beer with them. The Mexican lager is really the long-lost Vienna lager born again in Mexico. Lots of different people helped shape the Americas.

You can't go backwards, right? But I also think an apology would go a long ways, don't you think, Egon? Dialog with Spain and the Pope—especially Pope Francis—would go a long ways and could lead to reconciliation. We can't pretend everything was lovey-dovey cultural sharing. I don't think money will solve anyone's problems, like paying reparations, but who really knows, maybe it will. A reservation maybe? ... But what I do know is that the us versus them mentality never works because there can be only one victor, and nobody likes to lose.

Egon replies, I believe most people see that, too, Billy Bob, only they're overconfident that they'll be the winners. Billy Bob downs another mezcal and says, What's amazing to me is how an intelligent person cannot see the hypocrisy in it all. How so? Well, you can't have it both ways... Them pyramids had human sacrifices, even children sacrificed, with mass graves for the children. You see? You can't judge Christopher Columbus by the moral standards of today, just like you can't judge the indigenous people. Egon waves his head back and forth skeptically. Or at least we need to be honest about what all these cultures did and did not do. Sure, I'll take that, says Billy Bob. Egon admits, I've misjudged you Billy Bob.

Underneath your persona, you're actually a deep and thoughtful person. Billy Bob replies, I've misjudged *you*, Egon. You're a cool dude with some drinking capabilities. Another round of mezcal, por favor!

Egon lifts his hand toward Billy Bob, Tell me more about yourself. There is a lot I still don't know about you, Mr. Brewer and Restaurateur, and I'm sure you have a lot of great stories to share. You know, Egon, I traveled around the world so many times, I forget how many places I've been or even what I've done. One thing I do remember was the funny American stereotypes. Seems like Europeans view us as being improper and sloppily dressed, obsessed with instant gratification, always wanting fast food, loud, flashy, and rude along with being uncultured. Hey, my father is a hillbilly and my mother is a Chicana. My dad taught me how to be tough as nails and have proper mountain-man manners, and my mom taught me empathy and compassion. I think I represented us well in the Old World even if I wasn't what they would prefer to see.

Egon says, It's funny you can't remember. Most people make strong memories when they travel. Yeah, strange. Maybe I was warped somehow. I can't remember half the people I knew or even the women. I could never have a woman back then. I met women all around the world—in Moscow and Berlin and so on—and I was incapable of having a girlfriend. I have friends in Moscow and Berlin, but I can't remember their names. Something is wrong with me, I guess. Too many tours and missions scrambled my brains. I do remember my love for German beer and traditional German food. I loved the German Schnitzel and a traditional, unfiltered German lager. Who on this earth doesn't like a good German beer brat and pretzel with mustard, washing it down with a German wheat beer? Women I can't remember, but beers I can. They're my true love story.

You said you were incapable of having a girlfriend? That sounds sad, my friend.

I wasn't in a good place. I couldn't cry or show any emotion, especially love, and I filled the void with hookers. It's totally legal in most of Europe. I paid for women, and it became the only thing I could take. What do you mean only thing you could take? Well, I became dysfunctional. The only woman I could have was a prostitute, when something true came along, I shut down or ran away.

What made Margarita different? Or was it something else?

Margarita is a trooper. She doesn't give up. She showed me true love—that woman would cook for me like no other. Billy Bob, you're a funny guy. Well, Margarita can make tortillas better than anybody. She is the very best at Mexican cuisine. Spanish cuisine is always one of the top cuisines in the world, but the Mexican cuisine is one of the greatest gifts to the world and in my view the greatest cuisine in the world, with a perfect fusion of Old World and New World cuisines. Many influences for example, Spanish Chocolate and Churros, Indigenous influences with mole and tamales, Middle-Eastern influences such as Al Pastor tacos, French bread, Asian sauces to African spices all contribute to this new evolving cuisine. Egon replies, Now that is a lot of influences in a cuisine and don't forget about the Germans. Billy Bob responds, the German influences are undeniable although seems a little muted. The most obvious contribution was their fermentation expertise with cheese and beer. Egon says, Don't forget about the German influences of music such as banda and ranchera too. Immigration is one of the examples of what all the Americas have in common along with their contributions. I agree and sounds like a good woman you have there, Billy Bob. Yep, I agree.

So, you got out of the Marines, then moved to Juarez, Mexico. Well, I didn't go straight to Mexico. I had some detours. I have a lot of connections around the world that contract for world organizations. When I served in the 22nd Marine Expeditionary Unit, we took over a place in Afghanistan that people said couldn't be conquered—Uruzgan Province. Colonel Khan was our leader and spoke the Pashtun language and eight or nine other languages. Colonel Khan got out when I did, and he went back to the Middle East. I worked with him for a while and saved up a lot of money, then came back to the borderlands. I never tell people about that, Egon. It's a little too much, and I keep that stuff private. Egon asked gently, Why is that? To avoid the Spanish Inquisition! Some things are better left unsaid.

What did you say you did in the Marines again? I started out a Marine sniper then became an explosives expert. Did you see action as a sniper? What did that feel like? Billy Bob replies, Recoil. Egon replies, You say that like you're still feeling it now. How about being an explosives expert? That had to have been a stressful job. Sure, it's stressful. That's why I got out of the Marines. I felt my number would be up soon. You do too many combat tours and it'll eventually catch up to you. I needed a fresh start.

Suddenly Egon looks Billy Bob directly in the eye and says, Too bad about Chino killing those women... What? What are you...? Now way! No way it was Chino! You don't think so? Of course not! Then who? I don't know—you're the investigator guy.

Okay, okay, says Egon. I'm sorry to do that to you, Billy Bob, but this case is serious and I need to know who I can trust. Sometimes the ole surprise attack draws out information people hadn't intended to share. Billy Bob says, I'm beginning to wonder if any of you cops is worth the time of day. Don't be sore, friend. Listen, who do you think killed Fernanda or those other folks? It's baffling, señor. I don't have a clue. My instincts tell me it's someone who knew her well, probably intimately. Egon replies, Perhaps, but then how could it be the same person who did in Ms. Swallows or Ms. Mata? They were from out of town. You hire any new staff in the last few years? No, everyone's been with me at least four or five years, some a lot longer. Did you know Fernanda was found straight across from the Sun Brewing Motel on the Mexican side of the river? She had a note tied to her right hand. Lt. Wienke told me she was found in Mexico but he didn't give too many details. What did the note say? The note was on burned antique paper, written in calligraphy, and tied to her right hand with thin rope. Egon pulled out his notebook, found a page, and read:

I'm not even in disguise with you and I'm enjoying a beer.

Cheers to those big eyes you have while I read Shakespeare.

Walk with me and be safe.

Until I get to Grandma's place.

Billy Bob says, That's a creepy note. I'm sure you've got, like, scientists and stuff who can figure out where the paper came from and all that, right? Egon replied, Unfortunately, that's rarely so easy to do. We go where the evidence leads us, but sometimes the evidence leads to nowhere. Let's get out of here, Egon, and I'll take you to my favorite bar in all Juarez. Where is that? It's San Martin's. They have mariachis and buckets of caguamas. One of my nicknames from my friends in Mexico was Caguamon. Because you like drinking out of the big bottle, heh? Yep! If I had the opportunity, I would always purchase the caguama beer bottle, which is similar to a 40 oz. bottle in the States. Egon replies, It's all coming together now... San Martin's, mariachis, caguamas. Billy Bob replies, We can request some live covers of Vincente Fernandez. ¡Vamos, canijote!

You know, Egon, says Billy Bob, driving in Juarez would really throw a lot of Americans for a loop. Mexican drivers are aggressive, and they take their opportunities, because you never know how traffic could end up with all these millions of people. In a strange way, I feel a sense of freedom here. Egon replies, Why is that? Well, in the States it's rules for this and rules for that. Here, I feel like I could drive in reverse down the street and through the city and no one would bat an eye. Even the worst-case scenario, if I'm pulled over it's not the end of the world. In the States, you'll get fined for reckless driving and could possibly get your license taken away. The point is, you don't mess around in the States because the consequences are severe. I was pulled over on my Harley for not coming to a complete stop at a streetlight when there was no traffic or police around. The cops said they seen me through their street cameras. When the cops finally caught up to me, I was so far down the road that I didn't even consider that they were after me. There are an absurd amount of rules and regulations over there.

Egon replies, Yeah, there are many differences in our countries. Billy Bob continues, But it's the little things that get me. Egon interjects, It's the little things that get you caught! That's for sure, Egon.

They drive a few more blocks when Egon says, You know, Billy Bob, it dawns on me it's quite possible that I'm out bar hopping with a serial killer. Ha! You're a stand-up guy, Egon. I admire that, but on the other hand, you would have to be a little crazy to believe that. Maybe so. Aw, hell. The truth is, Billy Bob, I don't think you're a serial killer, but you're a suspect, and at this moment I cannot rule you out. We Mexicans investigate differently than you Americans. How's that? Mr. Wienke is all about the facts and how he can use them. I on the other hand want to know you. I'm not building a profile; I'm looking at you individually. Billy Bob replies, No better way to get to know somebody than over some Mexican cerveza with San Martin's buckets of caguamones, queso fundido, and tacos.

Egon tells Billy Bob, You know what I don't understand? It's the motive. On the surface there doesn't appear to be one. So many different types of people killed so many different ways. The location strongly suggests some commonality, but that's about it. You know, Egon, sometimes people are just firkin nuts. I'm not saying Porfirio did it, but if he had a mistress, that could complicate things. Egon fingers the rim of the window. You think your buddy had a thing with Isabella and Daisy? And maybe Mary, too? He's my wife's buddy, or my wife's friend's husband, more than mine, but no, I don't really think he's the type. Billy Bob, there's something else that bothers me. What's that, Egon? It doesn't appear to be a crime of passion. It's more premeditated and methodical in nature. I believe somebody's trying to outwit us.

{ 10 }

Chapter 10.

Dear Diary,

Often in the world, people present themselves as personable, charming, and wise. They'll say the right things and look good at first glance but if you peel away the layers of the onion, you'll see a more sinister side, a side that genuinely doesn't care for others. How is it that someone can do an act of kindness and actually be vain and selfish?

I guess charisma goes a long ways in this superficial world, but it won't stop Porky the Pig from being the main entrée at the dinner table.

Billy Bob is back home with his wife and kids. Journalists have been flocking around and asking questions even to Billy Bob's kids. Elias Rockenstein and Iker Casillas are outside Porfirio's house along with others looking for information. Porfirio is on the phone with Margarita, explaining that the international publicity is driving him crazy and that he is still grieving for Fernanda.

Billy Bob calls his kids together: Jesse James, a.k.a. El Guapito, and his daughters, Analisa and Natasha. Hey, kids, let's watch a movie together like we used to. Analisa says, Let's watch *Wonder Woman*! Natasha aks her dad, Why are you home? ...Shouldn't you be working? I'm taking a break from work, Natasha. I need to reset myself. Jesse James says, Let's watch *The Mighty Ducks*! The girls say,

No! Jesse James always gets to pick. Billy Bob tells Margarita, We're going to watch a movie! Can you make some popcorn, please?

Margarita brings out several bowls of popcorn; hers has fresh, chopped jalapeños. The kids are still fighting over which movie to watch. Aww..., says Margarita, My little Guapito wants to watch *The Mighty Ducks*, so let's watch that. Natasha protests. I'm going back to my room. Margarita says, Oh, no you're not. You stay here and watch a movie with your family. Jesse James is only 9; we can watch his movie. Analisa says, I'm only 13! I'm still a child! Natasha says, Well, I'm an adult, and I'm the only one who acts like one, so I'm going back to my room.

Before she can leave Billy Bob says, Natasha, you're only 16, a young adult at best, so don't get too uppity with your siblings. Now what's with all the war paint on your face, you going somewhere? Dad! It's not war paint, it's my makeup! I'm going out with friends later. Okay, but be sure to put some clothes on and don't go walking around in just a bra. OMG, DAD! It's not a bra, it's a crop top! Look at *you*, Dad! You're wearing a KISS T-shirt. You're more juvenile than anyone I know. Analisa chimes in and says, It's true, Daddy. Billy Bob shrugs and says, My loving family, huh? Margarita, did you put hot Cheetos in the bottom of my popcorn? Or was there just powder on your fingers? Hey, did you want me to make you a hot Cheetos-smothered burrito or my New Mexican–style enchiladas topped with hot Cheetos? I'll do it for you, you hot Cheetos monster, you!

Natasha sneered in disgust. Her father calls her over. Before you go back to your room, mija, everyone come over here and put your hands in the center. Now chant with me, Ducks! Ducks! Ducks! Ducks! Ducks! Ducks! Billy Bob, Margarita, and Jesse James start chanting quietly and grow louder until they're shouting. Natasha pulls her hand out as soon as she realizes what's going on, while Analisa rolls her eyes but keeps her hand in.

Natasha says, OMG, Dad, how many times are you and Jesse James going to watch that movie? Jesse James says, Hey, Dad, you da man, and Billy Bob says, No, you da man! Analisa states, That's misogynistic. What's misogynistic? You referring to yourself as the man. Billy Bob responds, Do you want to be da man? Ew, Dad. Billy Bob shakes his head. Teeny-boppers nowadays.

While I got you all here, Billy Bob declares, I want you all to listen up for a moment. I know you all know this, but let me say it again so I feel better. Stay away from strangers and be careful out there. We don't know what's going on in this town. That includes you too, Margarita. When you go out training for your triathlons, keep a sharp eye. And don't be afraid to tell journalists no. You don't have to talk to anybody you don't want to. Keep your phones charged and keep them on so mama and I know where you are. Don't answer anybody's questions, and if any problems arise, then call me immediately, no matter how small or where you are at.

The front doorbell rings. Billy Bob says, I can't believe this. What, did they jump the fence? He'd had a privacy fence installed around the whole property to keep visitors out and hadn't installed a ringer on the gate, yet. I'll be right back, everyone. Start the movie without me.

Billy Bob looks out the window and he recognizes Iker Casillas and Elias Rockenstein. He opens the front door and says, Come on man, not at my home. You know me, Iker. You should have called and left a message. I would have made you my special bologna sandwiches or Sloppy Joes. Look, we can arrange for something, possibly, but not here and now. Come to the motel tomorrow. Anyway, I'm not ready to give any information out right now because it's an ongoing investigation. Rockenstein ignores him. Are the Mexican authorities involved with this investigation? Billy Bob says, I'm not doing this right now, goodbye. Rockenstein keeps talking as Billy Bob closes the door. They're calling this person The Poetry Killer. Do you have any leads on who may be doing this?

Natasha goes out with some of her friends to the mall and she notices people are kind of staring at her and they seem to be talking about her. She also noticed a guy she liked stopped talking to her at school. Her best friend, Dreya, has even shied away from her a little bit.

Natasha and a couple of her friends are in line to go to the movies and a guy from her school comes up to her, shows her a crass meme about serial killers on his phone, and asks her, Are you the killer at your dad's brewery motel? Natasha started crying and left the line. Her friends caught up with her and told her to ignore him and go back to the movies. Natasha said, I'm so sick of social media and all these trolls and mean people. I'm exhausted. I've closed most of my social media accounts already and can't take it anymore. I'm just going home.

Natasha gets home and goes straight to her room and slams the door. Billy Bob and Margarita are in the living room, almost ready for bed. For Pete's sakes, what's gotten into her lately? Billy Bob cries. Margarita replies, She's a teen. She's going through a lot and needs room to decompress. She told me web sleuths are trolling her online and that she's having a hard time at school. Billy Bob says, Go give her some ice cream and a big hug, she'll calm down. She loves to have a girl's night with her mom to watch ya'll's chick flicks.

Billy Bob's phone rings, but he doesn't answer because he is always in love with his own ring tones. He ends up bopping his head to Atreyu's "Do You Know Who You Are?" This is one of the reasons Billy Bob never answers his phone. A text comes in next.

Margarita, he sighs, I was going to stay home tomorrow to try and finish editing my cookbook, but it looks like Lt. Wien-Key wants to talk to me, so I'll have to go back to work and see what else has gone wrong. I've got to do every single thing myself, it seems like. Maybe they caught the guy, says Margarita. Then we can put this all behind us. Let's hope so.

The next morning, Mr. Wienke is there waiting for Billy Bob with his trusty John John Coffee. Hi, Mr. Wiener-Key, says Billy Bob. Wienke whispers to John John, Billy Bob reminds me kind of a beatnik, doesn't he? John John nods yes. Wienke relies, Hello, Mr. Diddlesworth. And you know it's Win-kay. Billy Bob snorts and says, John John, write this in your notes for Mr. Leopold, please: My name is Billy Bob Dankworth and not Billy Bob Diddlesworth. Okay, now then, I'll call you Mr. Leopold instead, since you don't like the way I pronounce your surname. What can I do for you Mr. Leopold?

Leopold replies, I'm under a lot of pressure right now because of all these murders going on here at the Sun Brewing Motel. I'd like to catch the killer right now. We believe we have a profile of our killer. Billy Bob replies, Wow, that's great, what are we looking for, Mr. Leopold? Leopold said, The person we are looking for is an outsider. He's grandiose, superficial, and a narcissist. He most likely drives an orange Volkswagen beetle and has their own fashion sense that doesn't depend on social trends. He's not a psychotic killer or a revenge killer; he's an organized serial killer. You sound confident, Mr. Leopold. Sounds like you got it nailed down. I do, Billy Bob, and I wanted to let you know. Thank you, Mr. Leopold. Oh, one last thing, Billy Bob: You drive a 70s Volkswagen Beetle, don't you? Billy Bob replies, Yep I do. I absolutely love Volkswagens. What color is it? It's green, which is my favorite color. I guess that rules me out then doesn't Leopold? Not a chance Billy Bob. I'll be watching you! Watch all you want, buddy, you might learn something about minding your own business. I'll see you around, Billy Bob.

Billy Bob tells Peter, Gather everyone up and tell them I'm having an all hands on deck meeting right now. Everyone gathered in a corner of the bar. Listen up everyone, I know it's getting difficult because of all the negative attention that the motel is getting right now. In a strange way, it's boosted sales and turned this brewery/motel into a world famous—or infamous, rather—destination. But I also understand it's disrupting our lives, and I apologize for that. Private investigators, amateur investigators, all the news stations, the Texas Rangers, and all the international attention has really put a strain on all of us. I wanted to personally thank all you for staying the course and for your professionalism. We need to stay focused and stay locked in because we are under the microscope now and we have our annual Best Little Brewfest in Texas coming up soon. This place will be a circus, and some of best brewers in the world will be competing. Not to mention BDB2 will be attending this year. Benjamin D. Blackstone II is the proctor of proctors and the definitive word on beer. He's also the editor in chief at *The Brewing News*. I've known BDB2 for over a decade now; he's a retired NASA scientist out of Houston who turned writer about everything craft beer. He has over 200 medals himself for brewing and knows some of the very first craft brewers in the nation. BDB2 will notice everything and probably bring his trusty BJCP judge Larry Drinkawitz. We're going to put our white gloves on and make this place immaculate. I want the patio rocks to glisten, and I want the desert to look like a Zen garden. We need to have each other's backs and look out for one another because we are all in this together. Okay, I won't keep you any longer, but let's keep showing the world our world-class service and our world-class beer.

{ 11 }

Chapter 11.

Dear Diary,

Poetry is one of the few things that I truly love because it's how I express myself—all is right in the unaversive and it's like I'm fixed.

I came across a poem by Allen Ginsberg called Father Death Blues.

He mentions a lot of personified death but he also mentions a poor man and an old daddy and of course Father Death. As I kept reading this poem, the more layering of meanings I could see. I felt the spontaneous nature of his poem and how it contained his fears. I can relate to that with my own tears even while eating grandma's cookies.

But I couldn't help but wonder;

Did his tears truly ease his pain? ...or was his tears from something else?

Maybe they were tearful truths.

Maybe poetry is built on a lie?

Narrating not based on fact or reason.

We both could see the red sea of death.

I'm the poetry killer.

Or so I've heard.

.

The Best Little Brewfest in Texas is quite a spectacle this year. Thousands of beer entries for the competition and thousands of people attending, hanging out on the front and back patios and walking along the river drinking beer. Something about this event brings out people's flamboyance, lots of colors and outlandish clothing; it's like a big costume party for the world's misfits and outsiders. It's wonderful seeing all the locals selling their products, food trucks galore, and the general celebration of the love of beer. For Billy Bob, it's all about this Frank N' Stein hotdog stand streamlining his menu selling his BBQ dog, El Chingon dog, El Guapo dog, and corn dogs as well as his outdoor bar. He also has burgers from the grill menu like the Aye Wey Burger, Big Kahuna Burger, and the Spam burger. Since people are outside so much, he's only selling beer in cans and plastic cups.

This year has a different feel to it than normal because it has a circus-like vibe to it, including real-life clowns juggling down by the river and people pitching tents along the shore. The web sleuths are here in droves, some with signs and T-shirts that say "Justice for Fernanda." The news stations are out with their satellite vans. Benjamin D. Blackstone II—"BDB2"—and Larry Drinkawitz are here walking around sampling beer.

Chino and Peter pause a moment to look out at the crowds from inside the restaurant. What are they all here, for? Peter asks. For real, says Chino. It's like they hope to see someone get offed. Sure, says Peter, but what makes them so sure it won't be them? As Billy Bob says, People are firken nuts.

The awards ceremony is this evening, with plenty of catering and beer. The famous brewer Alice Cooper is even here and when Alice comes by, she always gets Billy Bob's footlong dog. Alice Cooper is the head brewer from her dad's brewery, and nobody can scarf down a dog and chuggle a beer as fast as her. She's kind of gothic and likes wearing black leather, and she's an expert brewer that usually wins something.

Alice finds Billy Bob and orders her footlong. They both are a lot alike in many ways and are good friends. Billy Bob and Alice decide to have a beer chuggling competition in public, but before they get started Billy Bob put on some music by the other Alice Cooper: "Feed My Frankenstein." Alice the brewer chugged her can of beer twice as fast as Billy Bob. They gave each other high fives. Billy Bob shies away from his heavy metal usually for his big events and will shift towards oldies and even a little country like Willie Nelson ("Pancho and Lefty"). He'll put Elvis back on, too, which is appropriate since there are a few people dressed as Elvis walking around.

Later that evening Billy Bob will pull out a moodier playlist he's rather proud of, featuring:

Dire Straits, "Money for Nothing"
Sam the Sham and the Pharaohs, "Little Red Riding Hood"
The Beach Boys, "I Get Around"
Bob Dylan, "Knocking on Heaven's Door"
Johnny Cash, "Riders in the Sky"
Neil Young, "Rockin' in the Free World"
Willie Nelson, "Highwayman"
Van Morrison, "Brown Eyed Girl"

For most of the day, however, he generally keeps it folk and oldies.

Margarita comes by and they all began to chit chat. Margarita says to Alice, I love the black leather outfit you have on. Alice smiles and says thank you; I love your dress. You look like a beautiful parrot or something. Margarita twirls and says thanks. Margarita tells Billy Bob, I just came by to see if you needed anything. I also went up front to see how Peter is doing, and he told me that we have been sold out of rooms for months. Billy Bob replies, Yep, it's been crazy, and thank you bonita. Margarita asks Billy Bob to walk her to the car. Sure thing, bonita. Excuse me for a moment, Alice. Billy Bob and Margarita begin to walk to the car, and she says, All Alice is missing is the gag ball, chains, and whips. Billy Bob replies, Maybe she has them in her room, darling. Margarita smiles and says, Well, be sure you never find out. I'm going home now; the kids are home eating pizza. Billy Bob says, Nice. Please tell the girls I'll make them my pizza with my special crust soon.

Rupprecht and Jon are talking with BDB2 and Larry Drinkawitz while sampling Rupprecht's eisbock beer. BDB2 swirls the eisbock in a tasting goblet, then smells it. Larry does the same and they both proceed to sip on the beer. BDB2 says the color is a beautiful dark copper color with red ruby highlights and excellent clarity. BDB2 also says the beer is malty and balanced with aroma that has a little fruit esters with a slight alcohol presence. Larry Drinkawitz says, Well done, Rupprecht, this beer has a pleasant mouthfeel of a smooth, warming alcohol presence that complements the full body and low carbonation of the beer. Shaman Barley and Teddy Bruski walk up to accompany their colleagues BDB2 and Larry. Billy Bob joins in too and says, I'll grab a taster also. Billy Bob gives some tasters to Teddy and Shaman so they can also enjoy. Billy Bob grabs a full goblet of eisbock and holds it up high and examines the beer's clarity, then proceeds to swirl the beer. Billy Bob tells Shaman and Teddy to join along with him step by step if they like. Billy Bob has a slightly different way of tasting a beer: He literally sticks his nose in the goblet and smells vehemently with his nose as far in the goblet as he can get it. Then Billy Bob looks in the sky to savor the moment and aroma. He then proceeds to not sip but take a huge mouthful of eisbock and as he swishes the beer from cheek to cheek in the biggest way possible like a saxophone player blowing out of one side of his mouth at a time. He looks around until he is satisfied to finally take the big gulp. Billy Bob then smiles and says, This is a firkin good beer.

The day goes on and people are getting a wee bit tipsy. It's time for the awards ceremony, during which Billy Bob himself presents the awards. People are taking their seats, BDB2 and Larry Drinkawitz along with other media get front row seats for recording, picture taking, and interviews. Billy Bob starts off by thanking everyone and by telling a few jokes while people settle in. Billy Bob says: Thank you all for beer-ing here. This event would be nothing without you, or at yeast without your beer.

Everyone is groaning but also kind of loving it. I'll make this quick, Billy Bob continues, since I'll probably need a potty break soon. You know, because IPA lot when I drink beer. But I wouldn't want to suggest that's a real problem. After all, we know that beer consists of ingredients evenly dissolved in water, which is to say that, technically speaking, beer is a solution. It's true! I believe beer is part of a balanced diet. In fact, you know how to have a balanced diet? Just grab a pint of beer in each hand.

Thank you, ladies and gentlemen! Without further ado, drum roll, please. Now for the triple gold best of show award presentation.

The winner is: Alice Saison from Gary Cooper Brewing Co.!

Alice and her dad, Gary Cooper, run on stage to receive their trophy and metals. Alice gives Billy Bob the biggest hug on stage as she is ecstatic. Gary and Alice take a bow as they receive a standing ovation, then exit the stage for a photograph and interview from Shaman Barley and Teddy Bruski, who works with BDB2 from the *Brewing News*.

Now that hundreds of winners and the grand prize winners have been announced and the presentation is over, people begin to mingle and celebrate. Peter comes over and makes an appearance and congratulates Alice and Gary. Peter says, I'm so happy for you, Alice. Hey, did you know a handsome dwarf needs a good Saison the way Cupid needs an arrow? Alice replies, You're so sparkly this evening, Peter. Alright, let's go have some fun. Peter says, Just because I'm sparkly doesn't mean you can take advantage of a handsome dwarf, Alice, but it's a deal.

Peter Francois Amador and Alice Cooper have a fabulous night together. They go for a walk down the river with some cans of brew. They even start to hold hands. Alice starts really falling for Peter, just as if Cupid put an arrow in her. She's known Peter for a while now and has always loved his charm. They come back and enjoy live entertainment on the patio; Ray Monroe was playing acoustical riffs all night. Alice has always liked Peter, but this was the night it all came together. The night winds down after hours of indulging in Tinnie and Amber nectars of the Patron Saints of Beer. Peter, being the distinguished gentlemen that he is, walks Alice to her room and bids her goodnight. Alice gives Peter a kiss, then she hugs him then kisses him again and they begin the kissing in the French style. Alice grabs Peter's hand and takes him into her room. Peter tells her, I can show off, you know. I used to be a fine gymnast. I'll back flip, then jump and hang from the chandelier, then swing like a monkey. Watch this, Alice! Peter grabs a can of beer, then drops to the floor and does the splits while chugging it. He rises and finishes with a smile, his arms wide open. Then he takes a bow. Alice says, Come here, my little Renaissance man.

The next day, Peter and Alice continue the honeymoon phase of their newfound romance and spend the day together, gallivanting around town. Around early afternoon, he asks her, Are you hungry, Alice? She replies, Sure, I could go for some food. Peter says, Let's go for a picnic! I have picnic baskets and blankets. I'll grab the nourishments for the grand feast. We can break bread together and be intoxicated with each other's warmth embrace. Alice replies, I'm already drunk in love, Peter.

Half an hour later, Peter and Alice commence their grand picnic. Peter lies on his side eating grapes that Alice holds above his head while he leans forward to bite. They lie down together, romancing the moment. It's as if nothing exists around them and it's only them two that matters.

They eventually make it back to the motel and start watching a movie together. They unwind a bit and Peter is walking around in his boxer briefs and she's wearing an extra-large T-shirt. They fall asleep for an afternoon nap. They awake and stay in Alice's room for a bit, and as the day becomes night, they go up the spiral staircase to the loft to enjoy the majestic Texas light show in the big borderlands sky. Peter says, I see the Big Dipper. Then he says, You know, I've never seen a night sky so magnetic. Alice says, How do you know it's the Big Dipper? Look for the brightest seven stars in the sky and connect them with your imagination. You'll see a constellation. See it? Yeah. It looks like an ancient brewing vessel with someone stirring the wort. What does it look like to you, Peter? To me, it looks like Elvis and Santa Claus drinking mugs of beer nog, but a lot of people see a ladle. A ladle? You know, like for serving soup du jour?

Alice asks, What's that building over there? That's Billy Bob's 100% Spontaneous Ale Project. He rarely lets people in there, and if he does it's when there is no brewing going on. He'll let people in when they're cleaning and it's sanitation time, though. Alice replies why do you think that is? Peter replies, Billy Bob tries to keep it only a terroir environment as much as possible. He's also a little superstitious about his spontaneous ales. What I find amusing about that, of course, is that he knows all the science of brewing spontaneous ales, but he also believes in evil spirits that will spoil his beer. He's the same guy I could picture using his baseball socks as hop boiling bags for good luck. Billy Bob will say, Do not touch the walls and do not touch anything unnecessarily, because it will affect the microbes in the building which will then affect the micro-flora in the air. He requires everyone to use a mask and hair cap in that building, and he himself wears a sanitized military gas mask. Men have to wear coverings over their beards, too. Alice replies, I love it! C'mon, let's go take a peak. You know Billy Bob would show me if he were here. Peter replies, Do you value my life so little as to ask me to do that? Oh, Petey, I could make it worth your while... Alright, then, let's live dangerously and do it. But seriously, be quiet and discreet. We are going into the forbidden garden.

Peter and Alice sneak over to the 100% Spontaneous Ales brewing building. Peter lets Alice in first, then he follows. Put your phone on silent and stay away from the windows. Here, put these on. They put on masks and caps. I'm one of the few people that have keys to the entire place. Alice says, You're really jumpy about this. Do you think you're being watched? Peter responds, Sometimes I do, now that you mention it. Alice responds, I felt we were being watched since the loft. Peter says, Do you want the lights on? Alice replies, Yes, please. Peter says, Okay, I'll turn them on briefly to see the place, then turn them back off. Peter turns on the lights but they are very dim. Alice says, This is kind of creepy, especially with the dim lights. There are custom shallow wooden vats in here, Peter explains. Believe it or not, Billy Bob prefers cement fermenters for his spontaneous ales, and he is transitioning over to that. This will all eventually be replaced with cement egg-shaped fermenters. Billy Bob isn't a huge fan of barrel aging, but I suppose he'll keep his barrel room here.

Alice says, There are a lot of fumes in here. Peter replies, You're right about that. There is a lot of fermenting going on in here.

Alice and Peter walk around a bit and make their way to the back of the building. Alice says, Did you hear something? Peter says, I'm feeling lightheaded. Let's go back to the front. They slowly make their way to the front, but then Peter stumbles and faints. Alice drops to the floor and tries to wake him, but he is non-responsive. Alice pulls out her phone and begins dialing 911.

As Alice dialed, she was stabbed in the neck with a needle and fell over, unconscious.

The perpetrator walks out the front of the building and Jon and Rupprecht, who had been disposing of spent grains behind the brewery, notice movement where there shouldn't be movement. Jon yells, hey! Who goes there! This person seems to be wearing a half face mask like something worn to a masquerade. The perpetrator glances over at Jon and Rupprecht and walks fast towards the train tracks, then takes off running full speed down the river.

Jon and Rupprecht go check out the spontaneous fermentation building and find Alice and Peter lying on the floor, passed out. Rupprecht tells Jon, Grab Alice and I'll grab Peter. We need to get them out of here. They pull them out of the building and call 911.

The police and paramedics show up within minutes and evaluate both Alice and Peter. Peter is given oxygen and awakens. Alice is being loaded into the ambulance. They'll both be transported straight to the hospital.

Jon follows the ambulance to the hospital. Rupprecht stays behind to answer questions from the police. The first thing they want to know is why they pulled the couple out of the building when it was a potential crime scene. Rupprecht explains, There's all sorts of CO_2 from fermentation in that room. Exposure for too long or in high quantities could kill someone. It asphyxiates you slowly and you die. I assumed they'd passed out. I thought she hit her head at first, but then I saw the gash on her neck with blood spatter.

In the emergency room, the doctor immediately evaluates her as Jon tells her what little he knows. He says one of his employees saw someone flee the scene. Given her symptoms and the history of things at that motel, the doctor says, we may need to treat this as a poisoning. She turns to a nurse and asks for an anti-venom. They put her into a medically induced coma, but at least she is still alive.

Chapter 12.

Dear Diary,
I'm getting reckless. I've been sloppy but the time is now;
I have refined tastes and I crave refined things—this is why I've created
my own my path. It's gratifying to be godlike. on second thought—I am a
God. Time for a sacrifice.
The greatest of all is supposed to be love. Alice and Peter struck through
the heart from Cupid—or was it a little devil? Love has abysmal depths and
is a complex emotion, that's why doctors would refer to me as a high-func-
tioning psychopath, or maybe I'm a sociopath that thinks I can love. But
it's all for love. What else is there? A great bloody opera of love...
People will love my grand finale.

Det. Pepe drive Rupprecht to the hospital. They go check on
Alice, then talk to Jon. He says, Doctor Holmes says Alice is lucky
to be alive. She thinks she was poisoned like the others. She's
worried about brain swelling, so they put her in a coma. It should
allow for her to fight back and heal herself. Peter is on oxygen in
the emergency room on the first floor.

The police, including Deputy Pepe, are investigating the area
back at the motel. Det. Pepe calls his son and says, It looks like
this may be another attempt. I want road blocks with checkpoints

everywhere within ten miles. Check everyone for any unusual odors, sharp objects, or carnival masks. Detective Pepe asks Rupprecht and Jon, Has anyone informed Billy Bob? They both replied, saying they've been calling him but no answer. I'll call him now. Detective Pepe calls Billy Bob, and he answers this time. Billy Bob, where are you? I was out riding my Harley with Mexican Mike, Arturo, Alonso and Chopper Bob, and now I'm at Chopper Bob's house drinking brewskis. Detective Pepe informs Billy Bob of what happened and tells Billy Bob to stay put and that he is on his way to Chopper Bob's home.

After Billy Bob was informed of the news, he immediately calls Peter and Alice, who of course don't answer. He leaves them voicemails to express his love for them both. He also calls Jon and Rupprecht back and they explain what they saw. Jon seemed calm, cool, and collected, while Rupprecht seemed really shaken up. They are going to meet back at the motel after he's done chatting with Pepe to go over what happened.

Detective Pepe and his son arrive at Chopper Bob's and asks where is Mexican Mike, Alonso and Arturo? They didn't come back with us, they stayed in Old Mesilla. I'll catch up to them after we take statements from both Chopper Bob and Billy Bob in separate rooms of the house. Detective Pepe tells Billy Bob, Start at the beginning, when you left the motel today. Billy Bob says, I needed time off from all the work put in for The Best Little Brewfest in Texas. I rode into work on my Harley Davidson in the morning, then left the motel around eleven o' clock to come here to Chopper Bob's. Me and Chopper Bob rode down the Camino Real to Highway 28 because we love to ride through all the vineyards and pecan farms on our way to Las Cruces. We always take a pit stop in La Mesa at Chopes for some New Mexican–style enchiladas and beer. Our final stop is Las Cruces to have a couple more beers before heading back. Detective Pepe asks, Where did you stop in Las Cruces, and what time was it? We stopped at Handlebars Cantina in Old Mesilla, around 2:30, I'd say. Whenever we ride to Las Cruces, it's usually only to Old Mesilla. How many beers did you have, and when did you leave? I had three beers—they were light, don't worry—and we stayed about two hours, then rode back on the back roads again on Highway 28. We finally made it back to Canutillo to Chopper Bob's house around 5 or 5:30. Detective Pepe asks, Have you been here the entire time after you got back to Canutillo? No, I called my wife Margarita and she said she had a therapy session with a client. So, I rode out to see her at her clinic to surprise her, to see if she wanted to go out anywhere or do any-thing. And what time was that? I think it was a little before sunset. Detective Pepe asks, What did you and your wife do? Billy Bob replies, She was already gone when I got there, so I took off riding out to San Eli to have some tacos and one final beer at Pistoleros Cantina and Grill, which is owned by Margarita's friend. What time did that happen Billy Bob? I think it was around seven. Pepe says, Then you rode back here to Chopper Bob's? That's correct, and that's when I answered your call. Do you have any proof or receipts of where you've been? Billy Bob gets offended and points his finger in Detective Pepe's face and tells him, I'm not the bad guy, here! You're insinuating that I had something to do with all this! I know how you guys work; you pick a suspect and do everything in your power to prove your theory right. Of course I don't have receipts! Who keeps receipts for a couple tacos and some beers?

Having given a statement to Detective Pepe, Billy Bob rides back to the Sun Brewing Motel to check on everything and talk to Jon and Rupprecht. Billy Bob expresses his gratitude that both Jon and Rupprecht are okay and for saving both Peter and Alice. They went over what happened again, and Billy Bob is really pissed off this time. Two of some of his favorite people in the whole world were harmed. Billy Bob thanks Jon and Rupprecht again, then tells them he has to ride out to the hospital to see Alice and Peter. Jon told Billy Bob that Peter woke up but has his phone off and is really sad that Alice is fighting for her life. Peter won't leave her side.

Billy Bob finds Alice's room in the ICU. Peter is there, and he's clearly been crying. Billy Bob gives Peter a little hug and tells him Alice will pull through, she is a strong one. Billy Bob purchased a book for Alice. He hands *The Catcher in the Rye* to Peter and tells him, Read this book to her; it was one of her favorites.

Billy Bob leaves feeling down and partially responsible without quite knowing why. He eventually makes it back home and is looking for his wife. Margarita is just getting out of the shower. Billy Bob Talks to her while she is in the bathroom drying off and fixing herself up for the night. He asks her how her therapy appointment went. Margarita grunts and says, They no-showed after all. That means they'll still have to pay me, but it is still a waste of time to go out there and wait for them. Billy Bob says, Well, I had a pretty horrible evening. Something happened to Alice and Peter. Oh, no, are they okay? Yes, they are, but I really need to lay on that sofa again and get a therapy session. Go and lie down; I'll be there in a minute.

Margarita comes into her office with her hot Cheetos and sits in her chair at her desk while Billy Bob is laying on his back staring at the ceiling. Billy Bob says, This is all happening so fast. I mean, it's been a couple years, but there have been so many attacks. My motel, brewery, and restaurant are getting sabotaged by all these murders, attempted murders, and the circuslike atmosphere. Margarita replies, while writing everything down, I understand. Maybe it's time for something new? Like what...buy a Winnebago and travel to Big Bend? Margarita's phone rings. She says, Excuse me for a moment, I'll be right back. Margarita returns and Billy Bob is snoring really loudly, knocked out on the sofa. Margarita continues to write more notes down, as she always takes detailed notes with every session with Billy Bob. Margarita kisses him good night and whispers in his ear, Everything will be okay, I'll make sure of it.

The next day Billy Bob wakes up early as usual and takes off to the motel first thing. He arrives to the motel to see Lt. Wienke and John John Coffee along with both Pepes. The news stations are there, too, along with Iker Casillas and Elias Rockenstein. People are camped out holding different signs and shouting for justice. Sr. Egon drives up, then parks and walks up to Lt. Wienke and greets everyone. They're all collaborating in the investigations. Iker and Elias are filming for KVIA-ABC local news and asking the investigators numerous questions repeatedly, like, Do you have any leads on the Poetry Killer? Do you think the Poetry Killer attacked Alice Cooper? Why does the killer choose the Sun Brewing Motel for his killing? As the news reporters are asking questions, you can hear people in the background chanting, Shut it down! Shut it down!

Billy Bob decides he's had enough already and tells everyone he's going to the hospital to see Alice and Peter. Lt. Wienke says, Only don't go far, and we'll be here when you get back. Egon asks Billy Bob if he minds some company. Billy Bob says, Sure, you can ride with me if you like. They take off in Billy Bob's green Beetle. Egon tells Billy Bob, I can see you're frustrated and having a difficult time. He replies, Yeah, it's driving me crazy, and it's all happening so fast. Yes, that's true. We've all noticed the murders, and in Alice's case attempted murder, are happening at an accelerated pace. Billy Bob says, And I'm afraid what will happen every day. All this craziness, and I have to prepare for my Valentine's Day dance happening next week. After that, no more events for a while and more security. Egon says, I don't know how you do it, Billy Bob.

Billy Bob replies, Keep pushing forward. I've worked too hard and come too far to just give up. All of this craziness will come to an end and there will be justice.

Billy Bob and Egon arrive at the hospital and stop for a coffee. Billy Bob notices Egon's order and says, Hey, you're like me when you drink your coffee. My wife, Margarita, puts all kinds of stuff in her coffee, and it turns into some kind of froufrou shake of a coffee drink. Egon replies, I drink my coffee the way God intended it to be drunk. Dark as the night is long. Billy Bob laughs and tells him, I like that. You know, the first business I was going to start when I was just a freshman in college, living in the dorms, was a coffee business. I was going to sell different blends of coffee beans out of my wooden push wagon in the streets. Why didn't you? I was a computer science major and discrete math was kicking my face in. I would spend hours trying figure out the proofs, and if it wasn't discrete math, then it was abstract algebra, and if not that, then it was something else like my artificial intelligence class, writing proofs using Modus Ponens theorem. So you were too busy with school to devote the time you needed to a business. That's correct; I felt my brain was going to explode, so I concentrated on classes and graduating. Egon asks Bill y Bob, What was your favorite coffee? The Mayan volcanic-grown beans are my favorite. It's something about the soil and how they cultivate it, but you know who does coffee the absolute best in the world? No, who? The Cubans, Puerto Ricans, and the Italians. Hands down the winners in my view. They are the people who inspired me in the first place with their good coffee. I consider coffee the second-best beverage in the world next to beer. Beer by far is the greatest beverage in the history of the world. Egon smiles and takes another sip. Here I am chit chatting with you, Egon, and trying to internalize in my head why this is all happening. Why would this happen to Alice, and how is she connected to all the other murders? Egon replies, That's what I'm looking for, the common denominator. Billy Bob says, That detective Pepe and Lt. Wienke are offensive, and they will try to pin these murders on anyone just to close a case and gain all the glory for catching a killer. They're not seeking truth and justice. Oh, I don't know, says Egon, but Billy Bob wasn't interested in professional courtesy. That idiot Detective Pepe asked me to provide proof of where I was the night Alice was attacked. I pay cash, you know? But he should get off his lazy keister and do some serious investigating himself. What was strange, now that I'm thinking about my timeline of where I was that night, was that my wife Margarita wasn't at her clinic when she was supposed to be with a client. I hate to say it, but it does make me wonder if she's hiding something. Egon looks shocked. You think she is cheating on you? Yeah, probably not, but who knows, really? Egon says, Well, I'm sorry to say it's not beyond the realm of possibility. We now know Porfirio was having an affair behind Fernanda's back. That's disappointing. Does that make Porfirio a suspect? Egon replies, he is not excluded as a possibility. We are still investigating him and others.

Billy Bob says, Okay, let's get up to the ICU. Peter is in Alice's room reading *The Catcher in the Rye* to her. The doctor comes in the room and tells them Alice is stabilizing and her organs are functioning. She is on track to be brought out of the coma tomorrow. I'm going to leave her for one more day, she says.

All gasps of relief, then Peter says, Thank God.

Chapter 13.

Dear Diary,
How bad can I be?
I guess like a computer—unfeeling.
It'll be in my poetry, transparent and revealing.
How good can I be?
I guess like a raven flying free.
It's time for ice cream and pork-barreling.
How fugly can I be?
I guess like my nubbly scars from snickersnee.
I'm cleansing in the flooding rain with glee.
I could smell it deeply as I opened up my olfactory receptors walking in the rain. It doesn't rain much in the borderlands but when it does it usually floods. I didn't bother with an umbrella, I just walked and walked and started singing in the rain.

Is there really any such thing as therapy to fix someone or is it really just treatment like putting on a Band-Aid? I guess the Band-Aid is a little comforting sometimes, thinking it's a part of the healing process.

Poetry embodies primeval mysteries of within and soothes my soul by this dark art form. Whomever coined me the Poetry Killer inspired me to become a better version of myself poetically.

DAVID SLOCUM

We all need to broaden our minds, but what's fascinating is how we do it, some use poetry and others beer. In my case both. If there ever was such a thing as therapy to heal the soul then this would be it and that would take courage, although a different kind of courage. Courage about the dark, to ask hard questions that are taboo.

What is beautiful anyways? Fake hair, fake teeth, fake smile, fake persona... I'll take the natural and perceived imperfections; now that's true beauty.

Alice all made up, who is she really fooling?

Alice and Peter sitting in a tree, k i s s i n g.

First comes love then comes marriage, then comes Alice with several midgets in a baby carriage.

>*As strange as it may seem, even a God has a code to try to abide by.*

>*I'm writing in my diary and the song Spirit in the Sky by Norman Greenbuam came on the radio. It's not often a song about God the savior is on a regular radio station.*

>*Maybe God is an atheist and a savior.*

Tomorrow comes as the sun rises and Billy Bob is out the door at the crack of dawn. He goes to the Sun Brewing Motel to check on things. Egon stayed the night at the motel and was sitting outside drinking a cup of coffee when Billy Bob drove up. Billy Bob notices and walks over to Egon and greets him. Guten tag! Egon replies, Buenas dias!. Billy Bob asked Egon how he slept, to which Egon replied, I felt like I was being watched, if you must know. Maybe Bianca was right and there are ghosts in this motel. I felt like that cuckoo clock was watching me the entire night. Billy Bob replies, Yes, that is strange. Egon asks, whose idea was it to put cuckoo clocks in all the rooms? Billy Bob answers by saying, I would love to take credit for that, Egon, but they were in the rooms when I purchased the motel. I've always loved cuckoo clocks, so I kept them there because they looked beautiful. I decorated the place pretty much myself based on what I already had to work with. It's kind of like cooking a meal with what you already have in the kitchen.

Egon asks, Who did you purchase the motel from? I purchased it from my wife, actually. It was passed down to her from her father. That's interesting. You must have loved her father. Honestly, I never knew my wife's parents because they passed away a decade before we met. Margarita always told me that her parents would have loved me, though. I'm sure they would have; you're a personable guy, though I could see how people would either love you or hate you. Billy Bob replies, Yeah, I have that effect on people. Why do you think that is? Well, you're a self-made man who doesn't care what others think, for starters. You don't fit the mold, and at the same time you run right against people's sensibilities. Billy Bob shakes his head. That so? I think you know it is. You don't hide behind your accent or live behind a façade. You are who you are, an entrepreneur, military man, and author who is a self-taught international award–winning brewer and chef. People hate your success because it puts a spotlight on their excuses in life. They also hate you for how you've done it, but they also love you for all the same reasons.

Believe it or not, that's what my wife says, too, but who takes time out of their day to hate? It's beyond me. I couldn't care less what other people do as long as it doesn't harm others. Egon reflects, Some people envy, some people lust, and some people are greedy plain and simple. Billy Bob replies, Is it so bad to envy someone's craftsmanship? Is it so bad to lust after happiness? Is it so bad to be greedy for the affection of your kids?

Egon cocks his head and leans back in his chair. Are you a religious man, Billy Bob? Billy Bob replies, I think so, I guess so. Maybe I'm more spiritual than religious, but I'm not sure... I do believe in God. The proof is simple: We have beer! That was meant to be funny, but it is partially true. But the real and main proof, my personal truth, is in seeing my kids grow up and being with them every step of the way. Egon replies, I can imagine no greater love than from a father to his children. But here's what I've learned from church: Envy is bad because it is the toxic desire to possess what someone else has—or for them not to have it. When you say "envy someone else's craftsmanship," that's not true envy. When you say "lust after happiness," that is not truly lust because it's not an abuse to want happiness. When you say "greedy for the affection of your kids," that's not truly greed because you're not trying to horde anything for your own power and advantage. You simply want all the love you can get from your kids.

Billy Bob nods and says, Makes sense. Egon says, So, last night I was walking around and I went into the front desk area of the motel and noticed something strange: The lights were off. Billy Bob responds, Yes, that isn't normal. Egon continues, But that's not all... There was a soft light coming out of the back wall by the floor. It was vaguely noticeable, but because the lights were off, I could see it. So, says Billy Bob, no lights at the desk but a light behind wall? That's right. What say we go take a look now in the light of day? Billy Bob replies, Sure, let's go.

Egon inspects the wall behind the counter, then they go to the back room, which is used for Billy Bob's office. Egon points to Billy Bob's book shelf and says, You have your own little library here. Lots of Stephen King and Louis L'Amour. Billy Bob replies, The best education I ever had was from a library because there was no schooling, but that's just me and my way of thinking. I try to get my kids to read more, but they are all glued to their phones and always on social media. When I was growing up, I actually knew the person's phone number that I was calling. I guess every generation had their problems... I'm generation X, we're known for being slackers and rebels without a cause. Egon grabs the book *The Sacketts* and a secret door unlatches beside the book case. Billy Bob says, Wow, I'm impressed. Nobody has ever found that secret door before. The area back there has no lights, but it's a small walkway with a little staircase to a door in the ceiling that goes up to the roof. Egon peers in and says, I'm assuming the door to the roof is locked? Billy Bob replies, That's correct. Egon goes in there and takes a look around but there isn't much room and not much to see; it's old and dusty. Egon climbs the staircase to the top and unlatches the door to the roof. There's no lock on here, Billy Bob. That so? When was the last time you were up here? I dunno, maybe years. I never need to get on the roof.

They climb onto the roof and walk to the edge to look at the sunrise over the Rio Grande. Billy Bob tells Egon, I'm about to head over to the hospital to check on Alice and Peter if you want to go with. Egon takes a lap around the roof. Fire exit in back here, he says.

They return downstairs, Billy Bob grabs a coffee, and they get in his car. As Billy Bob is driving, Egon asks, Why do you think there is a secret door to the roof? Why not a regular access door? Billy Bob replies, Probably just to be cool. I've always loved the secret bookshelf door, myself. We've got an access door back of the kitchen, too, but maybe the old man liked to watch the sunrise and sunset from the roof, so he put in a little getaway door for himself. Egon muses, Makes you wonder if there are any other secret passageways. I think I'd have found them by now, but you never know. You may have the world's most open mind, Billy Bob. 24/7/ 365, Egon.

They arrive at the hospital and find Peter and Gary Cooper in Alice's room with Dr. Holmes. Billy Bob sees that Alice is awake and he immediately goes over to her and says, Hey, Alice! Give me a kiss, darlin'!

Alice shrinks back and asks, Who are you?

The room went silent. Several seconds passed, then Alice smiled and said, I'm just foolin' with ya! I got you good, Billy Bob! Billy Bob gave her a huge hug and kissed her on the cheek. Peter hugged Gary out of a swell of emotion. Egon asked the doctor how she was doing and when she could leave. Dr. Holmes replied, She has made a remarkable recovery. We're just waiting on a couple tests, and then she'll be good to go.

Egon says, It's miraculous.

Billy Bob asks Alice, I know you've only just woken up, but do you remember anything from that night? Alice replies, All I want right now is to recover and start new with Peter. I'm scared of being a target, and as we've seen, tomorrow isn't promised. Tomorrow may never come.

Peter tells Alice, Let's run away somewhere. Some fantasy islands like Oahu or the Aleutian Islands. Billy Bob says, Alice, you wouldn't take my best host from me?

{ 14 }

Chapter 14.

Dear Diary,

Cupid is a magickal casuist.

A mystic in the dark verses of the occult.

To be Cupid is to be misunderstood.

It's Valentine's Day—life is sweet.

The harp is playing, let's have a treat.

I wonder if Cupid is really the devil in disguise, the little red guy with a pitchfork.

The ultimate deceiver and the king of fornication, or maybe not.

Maybe it's true love—does love conquer all?

It appears so, we've all seen beauty and the beast.

A carnivore hungry like the wolves, ready to feast.

Could Cupid bring me out of the darkness, playing the harp and shooting an arrow through my heart?

Cupid rides the lightning with his bident of power.

Little red magickal mystic with a fork, I'm looking for darkness, my natural habitat is nocturnal like an owl whoo-ing in the night, but every now and then there is a glimmer of light.

Who-who...

It's Valentine's Day morning and Billy Bob wakes up and gives Margarita a box of chocolates and a dozen roses. Margarita smiles and says, Thank you; they're lovely. Over breakfast, Margarita says, You have a long day today with your Valentine's Day Dance. You'll probably be out cold, snoring the house down, by sunset. No way, it's party till you drop tonight! Margarita asks, Were you able to release the two beers that I wanted for today? Yep, today is the release day of Rose of Maggie and Arrow for my Valentine. I was able to get them both done. It was good of you to want to name a beer after Maggie, he adds. She's been with me a long time and is really loyal. Margarita slowly smiles and says, I've had many good conversations with her recently. She deserves it. Well, I gotta get to the brewery. I'll see you tonight at the dance, Guapo.

Billy Bob arrives at the motel to start preparing for the Valentine's Day Dance and runs into Chino. How goes it, boss man? I wish I could say it was going better, Chino, I'll tell you that. You've been like my consigliere for a long time, now. I don't mind telling you that I've been having major nightmares almost every night. I just hope nothing goes wrong tonight. You know, nobody gets murdered. Chino replies, I know the feeling brother. I used to have nightmares in prison and long after I got out. It takes time, but you've always been a little paranoid, Billy Bob. That's just it, Chino. I feel like I'm in danger everywhere I go, like someone is after me. It's starting to consume me, to where I can't concentrate. Chino offers him a shot of mezcal. It'll calm you down, carnalito. Chino pulls out a bottle but Billy Bob waves it away. No mezcal? No, just not that bottle. Grab the other one with the scorpion in it. My wife gave me that for my birthday last year. It's as good a time as any to crack it open. They both take a morning shot of mezcal. You know, Chino, you've always been able to chug the worm, and sometimes when I take a shot with the worm in it, it gets stuck in my throat.

Chino just smiles and says, You don't have to worry this time; this bottle has a scorpion in it. You know what is also strange, Chino? What's that? I keep having this reoccurring dream. I can't make out if it's a dream or not... It's like if someone is talking to me while I'm sleeping and telling me, *Grandma always said, if you can't say something nice, then don't say anything at all...* and *How close are you to your grandma?* It's the strangest thing, then bang! Just like that I wake up and it's all dark and I ask Margarita, Did you say something to me? She usually ignores me or tells me to go back to sleep.

Maggie has been taking chairs off the tables and overhears a little bit of their conversation. That's strange you say that, Billy Bob, she says. Why is that? Because Margarita was just in here yesterday briefly checking on things, and she stopped to talk with me for a little while. She said the exact same things to me: How close are you to your grandma, and Grandma always said, if you can't say something nice, then don't say it at all. She sounded kind of strange when she said it, and she took out a bag of hot Cheetos and started eating them while talking to me. Billy Bob replied, That is a little funny. She was probably quoting me. Everyone knows I talk to my grandma a lot. Maggie replied, We know you talk to your grandma a lot, but we also know you're a little eccentric. Billy Bob said, When I talk to my grandma, it's not that I'm hallucinating or anything like that, it's more like I see her as an angel in the heavens. When I talk to Grandma, I look up into the sky to ask her for guidance, because she is my guardian angel. Maggie said, We've always known that about you, Billy Bob, but if someone doesn't know you, then they might come to the wrong conclusion. Billy Bob cracks a big smile and tells her, Thank you, darling, for saying that.

Billy Bob tells them, It's time to decorate this place for Valentine's Day. I want it to look hot with flames, hearts, and Cupid decorations. I've already put together my playlist. Maggie says, Let me guess, Elvis, Elvis, and more Elvis. Yes, ma'am, but don't forget Al Green, Frankie Valli, Tom Jones, and a lot of others, too. Chino, you got the updated menu with the new beers and food items, right? Yep. Billy Bob announces, We have three new beers in the lineup today: Cupid's Revenge, Arrow for my Valentine, and Rose of Maggie. Chino nods and says, Yep. Sheesh, Chino, Billy Bob laughs, you're starting to sound like me, now. The next thing you know, you'll be walking around without using curse words and saying *yep* and *nope* instead of using full sentences. Then Billy Bob gets really excited. I'm baking a huge Cupid cake today! It will be like a beautiful, colorful wedding cake with Cupid and his bow and arrow and lots of hearts. It's a beer cake with shades of red velvet and white cake, and the top layer will be chocoflan. I'll also have my special beer ice cream to go with it. We can also serve banana splits the old-fashioned way with my beer ice creams, topped with pineapples, my stout ganache, and strawberries. We also got fresh pecans from my biker friends at the Ramirez pecan farm. Special entrées for today are lamb shanks and fava beans, Cupid's Clafouti, paella, steak tartare, my chocolate bbq–sauced baby back ribs, Alabama white sauce beer-can chicken, Granny's Mac & Cheese, and my extra-large beer balls and jelly.

By late morning, the motel looks like it was decorated by a love-struck teenager, with lots of red hearts, flames, and Cupids. The tables have been moved to the perimeter of the patio to make space for the dancers, and Billy Bob has a computer and a couple speakers set up for tunes. The Valentine's Day Dance was Billy Bob's way of keeping that high-school first-love vibe alive with his wife, and it really caught on in town because it gave people a fun thing to do without a lot of pressure. People start funneling in for early dinners and are already having fun, dancing, drinking, and enjoying the good food.

A lovely group of people come in and sit at a table on the patio. Chino calls Billy Bob over. Boss man, look at 12. Is it me or do they all look like old celebrities? Yep, I see it. That couple there look like Jim Brown and Meryl Streep. All he needs is a dashiki! That other couple look like Meryl Streeps's twin and, what, Ken Jeong? Man, that's racist, Chino chides him. You don't think he looks like Ken Jeong? No, man. Tony Leung. Tony Leung? Yeah, man. *Hero. Shang-Chi. The Grandmaster.* Oh, man, says Billy Bob. Now, that's a great movie. Yeah, I see it now. You don't think they're potential targets for the Poetry Killer, do you? Bro, why'd you have to say that? Let's just keep sharp and try to have a fun, safe night.

Maggie comes out and greets them. She asks they guy who looks like Jim Brown, What's your name? I'm asking because you look like the legendary football player Jim Brown. He responds, my name is Charlie Brown and I take that as a complement, thank you. Charlie's girlfriend, Zsa Zsa Finklestein tells Maggie, I absolutely love your red blouse! Maggie smiles and poses and says, Why, thank you! I was hoping someone would notice. This is one of my favorite blouses, and I was hoping to turn some heads tonight. Good luck, says Zsa Zsa. Maggie tells the other guy, believe it or not, you look like a movie star named Ken Jeong. He responds, thank you, my name is Wang Kong Dong. Mr. Dong asks, Do you have vegetarian items? Maggie replies, Yes, we do, as she is passing out the menus. Just look for the arugula icon. Billy Bob, our owner and head chef, has a chilindrina or a caprese salad, and he also makes tofu sandwiches and shish kebabs. He also can modify some of his entrées. For example, his burritos can be made with rice and beans and vegetables and spices. The soup du jour is a tomato soup in a bread bowl, and that would be a good choice, too. The chilindrina salad has a little Mexican chamoy sauce in it, which originated in China and is similar in taste to a salty sweet and sour sauce but with a mild chili spice. The chilindrina comes with a side of chiles toreados.

Wang Dong's girlfriend, who turns out to be Zsa Zsa's sister, says, The beer menu looks fantastic. What is Arrow for my Valentine? That is one of our three Valentine's Day beers, released just for today. That particular beer is an American lager made with hibiscus. It has a red hue with a very subtle herbal tart flavor and a slightly sweet character from caramel malts that finishes dry. Marilyn replies, That sounds good to me; I'll have that. Wang asks, What is Cupid's Revenge? That beer is an imperial red ale that has notes of bready biscuits, caramel, toffee, and roasted flavors. It's a malty beer that is slightly sweet and slightly bitter, but it's not a hop-forward beer. It has a beautiful reddish-copper hue to it, but be careful with this one, it's very strong at 8 percent ABV. Wang looks around the table and puffs up his chest, That doesn't scare me! I'll have that one. Zsa Zsa asks, And what is Rose of Maggie? Maggie can't help blushing. That beer was named after yours truly. It's made with roses and hierba de vibora, which translates to *snake herb*. It has a very delicious taste combining a slight sweetness with an herbal undertone and a dry finish. It is simply magnificent, if I can say so without sounding biased. Zsa Zsa replies with excitement, Say no more! How could I pass up an opportunity to try it now?

Charlie Brown comments, It's interesting to see malt liquor on the menu. Maggie replies, Yes, Billy Bob loves his malt liquor. He's always pontificating how malt liquor gets a bad rap and that cheap mass-produced beers have changed the way the public looks at this style of beer. Billy Bob always says that people always fall for modern branding and think beer has to be one kind of thing, but that same beer is essentially the same or inferior to a good malt liquor. Jim asks, How so? Well, if you take the branding of a honey pale ale or lager that is 6 or 7 percent ABV, it could have a fusel alcohol burn to it and not be as well-crafted as his 7 percent ABV malt liquor, but a lot of people wouldn't consider it because of the stigma of being a malt liquor. His malt liquors are smooth and not watered-down, estery crap. A delicious, full-bodied, frothy, dry malt liquor. Charlie has a big smile on his face as he replies, Then I'll take the Canutillo Malt Liquor, please. Well, aren't you all just like a living advertisement for the brewery! I'll get these drinks up right away.

Maggie returns with their beers, then asks, Did you want to order food? Charlie replies, I'll have the Suffering Succotash and the Beer-Battered Fish and Grits. Wang asks for the Chicken Feet and Dumpling Soup with a side of fermented chamoy eggs. He explains, I'm on a plant-based diet, but I'm splurging tonight. Zsa Zsa's sister, Marilyn asks for the IPA Chicken Pot Pie, and Zsa Zsa asks for the Stout Onion Marmalade and Blue Cheese Burger and a Juarez burger. Maggie says, Wow, you're a hungry girl. I'm *starving*, says Zsa Zsa. She can eat anything she wants, says Marilyn. It's so not fair. Maggie asks Zsa Zsa, did you want beer-battered onion rings with that or sour beer-and-salt potato chips? We also have a side of brisket elote beer crinkle fries that comes in a large basket. She orders the beer-battered onion rings. Thank you all; I'll go put your orders in.

Margarita swings by and finds Billy Bob in the kitchen. Come out and dance with me! she says. I can't, darling. I've been thunderstruck with all these big orders and I'm in the weeds, but I'll catch up to you later, bonita. Margarita replies, I'll be in the presidential suite when you're ready. I reserved it tonight for Valentine's Day.

You got it, muñeca! I'll come get you after my shift and we'll party like the 80s.

Billy Bob brings Charlie, Zsa Zsa, Wang, and Marilyn their food. Marilyn said, So you're the famous Billy Bob of the infamous Sun Brewing Motel. Yep, that's me, and I hope you enjoy your meal without any infamy tonight. Zsa Zsa laughed and said, That huge chef's hat is hilarious. You look like the chef on *The Muppets*, except you're skinny and have that wolfman beard of yours. Billy Bob smiled and said, Thank you, I'm glad to make an impression on you. Zsa Zsa asks, Where did you get that lovely accent of yours? ...It sounds like you're a mountain man. Billy Bob replies, You're correct, ma'am. I get this accent from my dad, and they're all hill-billies on that side of the family. Billy Bob asks, Has anyone ever told you you look just like Zsa Zsa Gabor? She flaps her hand and says in an accent, Why, of course, they have, *dahling*. Hey, what kind of accent is that? asks Billy Bob. It's Franco-Canadian, my dear. I'm a princess or married a rich guy or something. Billy Bob says, Oh, right: another prawn on the barbie, hey mate? Zsa Zsa scoffs, Americans! That's Australian. Billy Bob replies, I know, I know, I was just foolin' with ya. I'll work on my sense of humor, Ms. Zsa Zsa. Oh, Billy Bob, you can call me Zsa Zsa, Zsa-Zsee or Ms. Finklestein. Will do, Zsa-Zsee Beetz. Do any of you need anything while I'm here? Is everyone good? Everyone has been laughing and enjoying the repartee. Charlie replies, All good, thank you. Billy Bob tells them, Thank you for coming to the Sun Brewing Motel, and enjoy!

Just then a flock of free-tail bats do a flyover, crossing in front of the sunset in spectacular fashion and giving folks quite the show.

Zsa Zsa looks astonished while Charlie looks frightened. Wang looks amused, and Marilyn says, I've never seen so many bats fly over like that. Zsa Zsa says, That was a perfect view, the bats in the sunset like that. Billy Bob had been about to leave when he saw the bats and then stayed to admire it all. Those are Mexican free-tail bats, he tells Table 12. It never gets old watching them fly by in the early evening or at night. I normally catch them around sunset because we are by the Rio Grande and the Canutillo Bridge. You'll see them flying around from time to time. They're majestic to watch. So free. Once again, welcome to my home. Enjoy.

The El Paso Elvis, known by day as Juan Carlos Maeso, steps up to the laptop and plugs in a microphone. Billy Bob hired him for a couple hours to sing some of the King's biggest hits for the dance. The El Paso Elvis is an old timer from the Second Ward, also known as El Segundo Barrio, in central El Paso. He's one of Billy Bob's favorite people in the entire world, an old man who retired from Sun Metro Mass Transit as a bus mechanic. He helped Billy Bob through several periods of his life, and they have a special bond. Billy Bob notices he's arrived and runs up to give the old man a hug. I'm so happy you're here, amigo. Thank you for coming. Juan Carlos is truly a throwback, an old timer and a very traditional El Pasoan. He is short, chubby, and has these huge bifocals that always look like they cover half his face and magnify his eyes extremely large. It's all part of Juan Carlos's charm, looking so adorable.

The El Paso Elvis sets up in the patio and starts singing all of Elvis's greatest hits. "Jailhouse Rock." "Hound Dog." When Juan Carlos sings, all the expressions in his face show you he truly feels it; his love for Elvis really shines through. He starts to sing "Love Me Tender." Zsa Zsa and Charlie Brown get up and dance to it. Wang and Marilyn join them, too. The dance floor is crowded with couples holding one another tight and gently swaying. Juan Carlos has all the hand motions and Elvis poses perfected and is always a big crowd pleaser.

Billy Bob ends his shift, does changeover, and bows out of the party early to meet Margarita in the presidential suite. He walks into the room and tells Margarita that he is in desperate need of a shower. Margarita has two goblets of beer ready to make a toast. Billy Bob grabs a goblet and says, I'll thank you later, bonita. Margarita says, Wait! Before you take a gulp...she raises her glass...Here's a toast to our future, and I raise my glass to *us*. You and me; no one can come between! Billy Bob says, I'll toast to that, and also to life's highway and doing it our way. They drink, then Billy Bob says, I used to know a clever toast, but here's a simpleton's toast, bonita: Cheers to your beautiful lips, darling. Our love is like a Shakespeare sonnet! And cheers to the bubblies in my beer. Billy Bob takes a gulp, then takes his goblet to the shower to drink it while he washes up. When he comes out of the shower, he dries himself off, puts on some boxers, and knocks out snoring, sprawled all over the bed, before he can even see the lingerie Margarita put on for him. Margarita sighs, smiles indulgently, and pours herself another beer.

Zsa Zsa, Charlie, Wang, and Marilyn make it back to their table to take a break from dancing and Maggie comes out to check on them. Charlie asks, Can I have a couple bottles of that malt liquor? I want to take some home. Maggie replies, Of course, I'll be right back with those. Maggie returns with two elegant bottles of malt liquor. Charlie looks astonished. I've never seen malt liquor in champagne bottles and everything, before. Maggie smiles and tells him, Billy Bob views his malt liquor as the true champagne of beer. It's naturally and highly carbonated and pale in color. Good beer is timeless and complex and deserves a proper bottle.

Wang has been casually taking in the view and the crowd and the motel. Then he looks concerned and says, That's strange. I think someone just popped their head up on the roof and then disappeared again. Twice. Maggie points up and says, Oh, that's just our loft. It's packed out tonight. No, says Wang, they were over there, on the far side, and it looked like they had a mask on. Zsa Zsa has been growing into her role the more she drinks and says, That *is* strange, dahling. Charlie starts laughing and says, I just seen it, too! Maggie looks up. Where? Charlie and Wang point to the far end of the roof where it's dark except for the dim light coming from below. Maggie frowns and says, That is a little peculiar. Probably just some kids sneaking around. I'll send someone up there. Wang says, You're right, probably nothing. Another round of beers, please!

Charlie says, You know, I can't wait to crack into one of these bottles. He takes the champagne cage off the top and begins to pull on the cork a little with his hands. It takes him some effort to get it about halfway, and then he takes a break.

Meanwhile, Maggie comes back with their beers and passes them out. Zsa Zsa asks her, Where did you get your lovely turquoise necklace from? Maggie smiles and says, I got it from the flea market here in Canutillo. It's handmade by members of the Native American Tigua Indian tribe from right here.

Charlie is admiring the label on his bottle of beer when the cork pops off and smacks Marilyn right in the eye. She cries out, and everyone at the table and around them freezes and looks at her, stunned and worried. Charlie and Wang get up and huddle around her trying to see if she's okay. Wang dips a napkin in ice water and gives it to her to hold to her eye. Marilyn is crying but insists she's okay.

When things finally calm down, Charlie gets up to return to his seat and stumbles over something. Maggie is lying on the ground. Oh my god! he cries and kneels down beside her and gently shakes her. Wang jumps out of his chair while clinching his fists in fighting positon. Then points at Maggie while yelling, Madafakas, she has a dart in her neck! Zsa Zsa is a nurse, and though she is slurring her speech, the adrenaline kicks in and helps her jump into action. She kneels beside Maggie and checks her wrist for a pulse and puts her ear to her mouth to check for breathing. She looks Wang straight in the eye and says, Call 911, now!

Something catches her attention, and she pulls a dart out from Maggie's neck. She looks at Charlie and Marilyn, and all three look up at the dark section of the roof. Charlie jumps up and heads into the bar, running right into Chino. How do we get to the back end of the roof? Hey, man, we have a problem on the patio to deal with. No, listen, we saw someone on the roof. Paramedics are coming to help her, and my friend is a nurse and is helping her.

Chino looks back and forth between the crowd on the patio and the back of the restaurant. Dammit! he yells. Okay, come on, let's go to the roof. He leads Charlie across the patio to the motel side, then up some stairs, and out onto the roof. They turn on their flashlights on their phones and search all over but can't find anyone. Where could they have gotten out? maybe jumped to that tree over there, Charlie asks. Unlikely, says Chino. There are usually people in and out over there. But it's dark behind the motel, Charlie says. Good point, the stairs are more visible.

They walk to the edge of the roof and look down toward the patio. The red and white lights of an ambulance are flashing against the night sky. They're hooking her up to an IV and have the defibrillator pads out. There's a bunch of shouting, guests are crying. Billy Bob shows up in his boxers and has to be restrained from running to Maggie. Then all the activity suddenly stops and it grows eerily quiet. Chino begins to cry. Billy Bob falls to the ground.

Someone covers Maggie's face with a white linen napkin.

{ 15 }

Chapter 15.

Dear Diary,

I spy a brewing ingredient with the letter C from the cornfields of La Union, New Mexico.

Corn from the magickal cornfields... that you love to brew with.

You are going to need a magick trick to keep brewing with this one.

Maybe you'll put your Houdini hat on, but it's only an illusion, that's why you'll fail.

It's amazing how two become one, we've become so alike.

I was never the prodigal son or a buckaroo like you but I have virtues as well, even though they were never on your list.

I'm a great brewer too but we were never meant to coexist forever.

You have my heart to the last number...

We need a new start.

Like songbirds in the cornfields, but for you nevermore.

It'll always be you that I adore.

Sometimes I feel like I'm an alien on Mars—maybe I'm Marvin the Martian with my space modulator ready to blow up the outside world. I guess only a looney tune would be capable of doing such a thing.

Maybe love and hate are intertwined forever—you can love and hate the same person after all. What a paradox, love and hate. I do everything *for you and give you everything, even my freedom and for that I was never able to be myself. Imagine my vulnerabilities... I've tried to tell you, for you to see the real me. You are not the only person who shows their real colors. In the end our true colors always shine through. I do love your fortune and fame, your animal magnetism and courage but I hate you for loving me. I hate you for always challenging me, correcting me and trying to make me feel inferior to you all the while eating your steak like a caveman, gulping beer and belching as if when you do it it's sophisticated. You do all this and have the audacity to call me rude. Then I call you out on your hypocrisies then you openly admit, I'm rude, crude and socially unacceptable.*

I hate you for loving me and it's too late now.

The only way out is to set me free.

Detective Pepe and Lt. Wienke take statements from the usual folks. Collaborative investigations ongoing. It was a freak show before, but now it's a full-blown Barnum & Bailey's Circus. Murder: The Greatest Show on Earth. People from all over the world make the trek to the Sun Brewing Motel to see the place where the one they call "The Poetry Killer" does his nefarious work. The Rio Grande is filled with RVs, vans, and people pitching tents. Some of them sell arts and crafts from small booths. You have clowns juggling for entertainment and for money. Web sleuths and amateur investigators filming with their phones along with all the news stations vans camped out.

There is a cult theory among a small group of fanatics that the Poetry Killer goes after women who have spurned him because he's such a passionate lover. Some of these folks, almost exclusively women, have camped out just on the edge of the motel property. They put signs on their tents reading: Poetry Killer, Take me with your Poems.

Investigative reporters from all over the world seem to be poking their noses into every nook and cranny of the motel. The Texas Rangers and local authorities are constantly in and out, too.

Billy Bob can hardly function in the face of this latest monstrosity. Grief for his long-time friend and co-worker nearly overwhelms him. He called her parents, but they did not want to talk to him. They told him they would make the funeral services public.

In the midst of all this, Billy Bob's cookbook finally comes out. He was supposed to have a big book signing at the restaurant soon after Valentine's Day, but they are able to push it back a few days to let some of the furor die down. When the big evening finally arrives, the place is packed with all the out-of-towners hoping for something exciting to happen.

Billy Bob looks out from the kitchen at the crowd hungry for blood. A banner hangs next to a table with a big picture of the book, a bright yellow and red cover reading, *The Sun Brewing Motel Cookbook: Avant-Garde Brewing and Cooking from the Texas Border.* But he knows they aren't there to hear about how he makes his spontaneous fermentation breads and ales.

For the first time in his life, Billy Bob contemplates hanging up the gloves and calling it quits. It's extremely hard to do and it's hard to explain really why. Billy Bob has accomplished pretty much all there is to accomplish and always loved his work, never even thought of retirement before, never backed down from any challenge. He planned on working at the Sun Brewing Motel for the rest of his life. But playing host to a serial killer was not part of that picture.

He knew when he showed up that morning that his head wasn't in the right place, but his agent and the local bookstore were insistent that they couldn't move it back again and it would only make things worse if he canceled. So he made the rounds at work to make sure things were running properly. Brewing and cooking always helped to wipe away all the worries of the world for him. The first thing he checked on was the brewery. He's slowly given Rupprecht more responsibility, and he thinks he could probably turn most of the brewing over to him if he needed to. As long as Rupprecht could brew one of his own recipes once in a while, he'd tolerate Billy Bob always seeming one sided.

In the brewery, Billy Bob checked on the Cornhusker Lager and A Book & Inoculum 100% Spontaneous Ale, which have both been bottle conditioning and are due for release soon. Cornhusker Lager is a special bottle release made with the magical corn from the cornfields of La Union, New Mexico. It's an American lager made with a cereal mash combined with a decoction mash to give it a unique mouth feel and body. The 100% Spontaneous Ale is a true labor of love that takes an incredible amount of patience and often times a little luck to pull it off. The Patron Saints of Beer need to be smiling down on you for good fortune with a beer like this because of the unpredictability of it all. That's what makes it even more special and the reason why only a handful of breweries in the world even attempt a beer like this. A Book & Inoculum is a 5-year aged beer that has matured magnificently. Billy Bob will fight anyone who contradicts him when he insists that beer judges haven't truly caught on to the nuances of a beer like this. It's the prime example of esoteric, he always says, and you can't fit esoteric into a neat category.

Both bottle releases were good to go, so Billy Bob made his way to his kitchen to go over the specials of the day. They have a stout beer–roasted pheasant with carrots, parsnips, and red onions, served with corn on the cob from the cornfields of La Union, New Mexico. The soup du jour is Rabbit Brunswick Stew. Billy Bob helped with the preparing, getting everything in place and overseeing everything. He doesn't think of himself as a micro-manager, but he is also convinced the motel and restaurant would fall apart without him. Peter and Chino are great, but any time he turns the reins over to them, they bring a different flavor to the place that just isn't what Billy Bob wants for it.

People start funneling in for the book signing, but Billy Bob hasn't set up his table yet with his author copies of his book and his bottled beer releases. Billy Bob smiles and greets people the best he can. Chino brings out a table and sets it up on the patio. Billy Bob grabs a couple boxes of his books from his office and puts them under the table, then pulls out a bunch and stacks them up. Peter, who has fully recovered, takes a book and stands it on its end so everyone can see the cover. Rupprecht and Jon bring boxes of Cornhusker Lager and A Book & Inoculum 100% Spontaneous Ale to the outdoor bar. Peter takes a bottle of each and adds them to the display.

Billy Bob gets the crowd's attention and explains the special releases to them. He encourages them to get a Cornhusker to drink tonight and a Book & Inoculum to enjoy on a special occasion at home. Once he gets his area setup, he cracks open a Cornhusker Lager because it's light and refreshing. The beer is designed for the long haul, like barbecues, picnics, or concerts, where the 100% spontaneous ale is more of a beer you sip on around a fireplace. Plus, Billy Bob wouldn't open A Book & Inoculum unless it was for a really special occasion where he could enjoy it in solitude and silence, maybe with Margarita by his side. It's just not his style for a book signing among the masses.

Billy Bob finally gets up to begin the event. He makes eye contact with Margarita, who has just arrived and is standing in back by the bar. She smiles and nods to encourage him, which he appreciates. He reads from the introduction to his cookbook.

It describes his Southern comfort, soul-food, Tex-Mex, and borderland cultural upbringing and his passion for brewing, cooking, and experimentation. He points out that everything in the book has been served at the restaurant, and a lot of it is still on the menu, so if they have a favorite dish they can make it at home, or they can try it in the restaurant first. After a couple questions from the crowd, Peter explains how they can buy the book and get it signed by the author. Billy Bob cracks his knuckles, gets a fresh pint from Chino, and prepares to spend the next hour or so writing his signature and making small talk. The line is long and like a zoo with all the different personality types that have shown up. Some of the people are offensive, intrusive, and insensitive while others are appropriate and civil. Some are chill and some are highly animated. The new server, Camelia, is working the line, taking orders, and delivering beers while people wait. It's a great night for business and for his book, but Billy Bob is truly an introvert and would prefer to be hiding in the kitchen.

From the front of the building people can start to see red, white, and blue flashing lights. Several police officers walk around back and take up positions surrounding the patio. The ABC news crew is already out and filming, and the web sleuths are scrambling to find good positions. Both Pepes and Lt. Wienke approach Billy Bob at his table.

Excuse us, folks, says Wienke, waving the crowd back. Sorry to break up the party, but Billy Bob, you are under arrest for the murders of Maggie Sanchez, Fernanda Escobedo de Diaz, Rigoberto and Mary Del Toro, Daisy Swallows, and Isabella Mata.

The crowd gasps and breaks out in a flurry of concerned and frightened conversation. Cameras are going off everywhere. Billy Bob jumps up as if he's going to run, but the Pepes draw their pistols. Don't get brave on us, says Pepe, Jr.

The Brewers' Murder Diaries

I'm not running! I'm not running! says Billy Bob. But you guys got this way wrong. I'm not your guy.

Lt. Wienke nods to an officer, who comes up and handcuffs Billy Bob while reading him his rights. Everyone is floored, and some in the crowd even begin shouting at the police that Billy Bob is innocent and to leave him alone. Margarita tries to run up to him, but another officer stops her. Det. Pepe says, It's all right, let her see him before we take him away. She hugs him tight. She's afraid but not crying so much as growing angry. It wasn't me, he tells her. I know, baby, she whispers in his ear. It wasn't me, he keeps saying. She puts her hands on his shoulders and looks straight in his eyes. Then moves closer to whisper, I know, baby. It wasn't you, it was me.

Billy Bob was unsure if he heard her correctly, there was a lot going on and he was in shock. Something about her tone strikes Billy Bob as curious, too certain, or hiding some other meaning that gave it a strength but also a dangerous edge. His mind went to work on the problem, until a horrible possibility presented itself. The question rose to his eyes to confirm what he thought she whispered in his ear, and she saw it, and her face became serious as if to say, *Say nothing!*

As they lead Billy Bob away, he keeps turning back to look at Margarita with an expression of confusion, sadness, fear, and distress. Her nostrils flare as her eyes say again, *Say nothing!*

Billy Bob was taken to the interrogation room and made to wait for hours upon hours. At some point he put his head down on the table and dozed off. It was still dark when Lt. Wienke entered and offered him a soda pop or something to drink. Billy Bob didn't reply. He just sat there, eyes glazed over, like a lion caged and defeated.

{147}

Wienke tells Billy Bob, I am legally required to draw your attention to that camera on the wall. We have been recording everything since you were thrown in here and we're recording now while I get some answers from you. Billy Bob moves only his eyes toward the wall where the camera is. Whether or not he already knew it was there isn't clear.

Wienke leans on the table and glares at Billy Bob. Why did you murder all those people? Billy Bob looks hurt. I didn't do it, Wienke. This is all so messed up. Someone is targeting me or the motel. Wienke fires back, Who? Who is targeting you? After all this time you suddenly remembered an enemy with the means and motive to do as he pleases on your property? As he talks, his voice gets increasingly louder and more strained and starts to sound squeaky. Who is targeting you, Billy Bob! Billy Bob replies, Man, I don't know. You don't know? No kidding, you don't know—because there isn't anyone! You are the Poetry Killer, you sick puppy! All these murders are tied to the Sun Brewing Motel, and you killed them all! You were on the property every night, you know the secret doors and tunnels. Shoot, you even showed up soon after some of the bodies were found. And how many people do you know could hit a target in the neck with a dart gun from 75 feet away? Don't tell me it was Peter or Chino.

Look at this. He dropped a file folder on the table. We had the FBI work up a detailed profile of this Poetry Killer, and wouldn't you know it matched you perfectly, Billy Bob! An outsider living by the beat of his own drum, kind of like a beatnik. Keen senses, especially smell, probably delusional about his own capabilities and importance, and driving a Volkswagen Beetle.

Billy Bob starts getting agitated. Listen to me, gull darnit! We been over this: You got the wrong person! I have a *green* Beetle and your file says you're looking for an orange one. And, yeah, maybe

I'm different, but I'm not delusional. You think it's good business to go around killing your wife's family or any woman who bats an eyelash at you? Your FBI profile is stupid. Talk about police profiling. How can you be so bad at this? No wonder people laugh at the FBI. For crying out loud, that guy standing out there had an FBI T-shirt on, and you have a *Walker, Texas Ranger* T-shirt on. You're a bunch of kids playing cops and robbers. Wienke looked down at his T-shirt and got angry, Don't you dare talk about Chuck Norris! Billy Bob yells, At least Chuck Norris always got the right bad guy!

Oh, I've got the right bad guy, says Wienke. I got him because he wanted to get got. What are you talking about you dime-store cowboy? Look at the last six beers you've released:

Meados de Alien Ale, released right after Isabella Mata's murder and brewed in the same cement fermenter that Isabella was found in. You sick puppy, you! I know what Meados de Alien means in English; it means alien piss! Isabella was a Mexican national, you prejudiced racist.

Cinderella Loves Ale. Right after the Daisy Swallows murder, you psychopath. You're sick, Billy Bob, real sick, and I'm going to make sure you're locked up for life.

Rio de Piedad Ale, right after Mary and Rigoberto Del Toro were found in the Rio Grande. You even advertised how you used river water from behind your brewery as an ingredient. Who would name a beer "River of Mercy" right after a double homicide in that river? I'll tell you who: It's you, Billy Bob! You're full of yourself, but I think you're full of it! I speak a little Española too, Billy boy!

Fernanda's beer you named after your victim in plain sight based on her perfume. Did you think nobody would notice your twisted and sick souvenir trophies?

Arrow for my Valentine and Rose of Maggie! You made a beer named Arrow for my Valentine then shot an arrow in your own employee's neck. You even dedicated a beer to her called Rose of Maggie before you did the deed, you sick antisocial sociopath.

And now A Book & Inoculum Ale at your book signing event. Narcissist that you are, you named your most prized beer "inoculum" when we know you smuggle black market scorpion venom and poison your victims with it.

I've never liked you, Billy Bob. You're vain, smug, and a stupid wannabe frontiersman. Yeah, I said it. Just try and come at me. I don't like your kind, and it's time for justice, Texas Ranger style. I've got your name, I've got your number! You slimy walrus! You were the only one who had access to the fermenter that Isabella was found in. You disappeared right before Maggie was shot by someone with access to the rear of the roof. You know how to tie knots and use boat rope like what Daisy and the Del Toros were found tied with. You are the Poetry Killer, and you kept your liquid poetry in those bottles for victim souvenirs! No more rising suns for you, Billy Bob. We are going to charge you to the fullest extent of the law and seek the death penalty.

Billy Bob replies, Listen to me, you big dummy! I always keep it straight 100. That's the only way I know how to be. You line up a series of coincidences and thoughtful deeds and twist them to look like some sick joke. I'll have you know that frontiersman are some of this country's most independent, strong, resourceful, friendliest, least greedy people you could ever hope to meet. You'd never find them locking up one of their own just to get the glory of catching the Poetry Killer. Where's the justice in that? You're going lock me up and charge an innocent person with some cockamamie case about killing his own guests, and all for what? You miserable baggage. If anyone should be locked up for life, it's you Leopold Wiener-Key.

Let's go, Billy Bob. You're staying at *my* motel, tonight. I have to apologize, though, the doors and windows are all barred up. You understand.

Chapter 16.

Dear Diary,

Here I am in a jail cell writing in my diary nonstop trying to pass the time. Chino came by to see me today and I told him that I don't think I can handle a cage. People are calling me Bloody Bill in here. I also told Chino that I'm not the serial killer of the Sun Brewing Motel, I'm not the Poetry Killer. People just say, Yeah right, that's what they all say. Chino said, I know, carnalito. I believe you. I know you didn't do these things. I've known you a very long time bro, I know you. I've never met someone like you before, definitely not as crazy, but I know you're not the serial killer. You are crazy, Billy Bob, but you're also a very good person. I told Chino, I don't think I'm going to make it, I'm not going to be able to handle a jail cell. Chino told me, Hang in there, brother, it's not over yet.

I told Chino, I've had a long time to think about my life while being in a jail cell. I'm not the Poetry Killer, but maybe this is payback. I've done a lot of bad things in my life, and this is just poetic justice. I'm paying for my sins of the past, so in a sense I deserve it. Chino replied, You're wrong, Billy Bob. I told Chino, I've done a lot of things I deeply regret, and I tried to put it behind me. I guess this is my reconciliation. There was a time that I often wondered why I felt nothing, no emotions—then I came back to the borderlands, I started anew, and it changed my life. Some of the things

I've done overseas, I'm not proud of. I also was incapable of any kind of relationship, I preferred hookers and detachment because it was natural for me. Chino told me, You done a lot of good in your life too, to which I replied, Yes, I know, but it's the bad that I struggle with. I'm okay with paying for my sins now in jail. We all pay our debts sometimes.

I was debating on telling Chino this, but I told him that I suspect Margarita is the real Poetry Killer. He looked at me, expressionless. How and why could my wife be the serial killer? I tried to understand it. Was it my money and possessions? Did she have some kind of secret personality that no one suspected? And what was I supposed to do? The woman I loved did all these horrible things...

Chino said, No offense, bro, but I always thought something was a little off with Margarita. When you've been around for a while, especially around insane criminals in prison, you kind of figure people out, especially these psycho types. It's something in their eyes, like they're always daring you to call them out. I'm going to get you out of here, Billy Bob, he said. Right now you're going through a hard time in jail, but prison will change you permanently as a human being. It will make you inhuman.

I asked Chino, If that's true, then how did you turn out to be such a standup guy and my best friend? Chino replied, I am a standup guy, but I'm really crazy and I recognize crazy, just like I recognized it in you many times. Just like when we were riding through central El Paso with our wigs on, drinking beer and about to get into an all-out brawl. The difference is that I'm changed for life in a terrible way on the inside. I'm changed on the outside, too, but you wouldn't be able to see it too much. Chino went on to tell me, I've always noticed you've had PTSD, I've just never said anything about it. I told Chino, No more therapy sessions about the life and fast times of the Sun Brewing Motel. Now I'm in jail, and I really don't think I'll survive. I never really liked to talk about my personal stuff, and I assumed it was the same way with you, but I'm going nuts in here. Chino replied, You are right about that.

Chino told me that he had to go now but he would be back. I said, Whatever you do, leave Margarita out of it.

He also told me: You are my friend. I'll do anything for you. Love got you in here, and love will get you out.

Chapter 17.

Dear Diary,

Seems like there is no place for multiculturalism in jail. This is kind of funny. It's actually really funny. I look like a beatnik Caucasian with a soft Southern accent, but I'm also Chicano, a multi-cultural mutt. Someone like me really doesn't fit in. There are nothing but tribes here. Everyone has gone tribal and only stick to their own kind. One thing for sure is that I can't appeal to everybody, but I do speak Spanish.

I remember Lt. Wienke asking me, What's wrong with you? ...You're a redneck hillbilly and acting all Mexican. I didn't know how to respond. I grew up on fried chicken and tamales. I yam what I yam. I don't fit in anywhere, and I never knew how strong I had of a country accent. I see farmer Mexicans and different rancher folks all the time everywhere I've lived, but it didn't dawn on me that I was really different fundamentally. All of these prejudices are now coming to light on me and in a hard and fast way in here.

This is a real living hell—no mariachis, no cervezas, and no fried chicken. If there was ever a 6th sense for taste, it would be fried chicken. I actually invented the I Heart Fried Chicken bumper sticker. What I wouldn't do for a huge box of Granny's Southern fried chicken right now. You don't know how good you got it until your freedom is taken away.

Everything in a jail cell is an escape in my head. I can take myself anywhere in my mind. I can hear Johnny Cash singing "A Boy Named Sue" in my head. Like Andy in Shawshank Redemption. *I look up and smile, thinking Grandma loved Elvis. Maybe I'll play "Jailhouse Rock" next in my imagination. Coping with life in jail is all an escape in some fashion. I think seeing the sick humor in things or seeing the humor in any situation is a survival instinct. "Love and War" by Drowning Pool starts playing in my head. Time to switch the music in my grape to some Fear Factory, "Invisible Wounds." It's time to turn it up a notch to some Atreyu, "Portrait in Black" and some Killswitch Engaged, "Untitled and Unloved." All I have in jail is the music and the voices in my head. I can escape anywhere.*

My wife came by to see me today. It was so confused. She pranced in all high and mighty, all malicious smiles like a supervillain. I had to know the truth so I asked, Why'd you do it? Was it some kind of jealousy? You've ruined everything. She said, Can you see the hot Cheeto powder on my lips? Anyway, don't kid yourself. Jealous of you? Everyone knows I'm too good for you, baby.

Why are you talking like this? I don't understand. Bonita...

Stop calling me that. This farce is finally over. Once they find the diary, it'll be the last nail in the coffin for you.

I told Margarita, I just want to know why you did it. You were my everything, my lover and my best friend. When I fell in love with you Margarita, I seen the stars dancing on the water and your beautiful face painted in the borderlands' pink and purple sky.

Margarita snapped, Oh, don't be a fool! Anyway, I only came here to let you know I won. I was the only one close enough to you to bring you down. At least they didn't die in vain. I was in disbelief and could hardly talk. Didn't die in vain? Margarita replied, It was for the greater good, just be thankful I spared your life, which you'll get to spend in prison, no doubt. Don't worry, I'll take care of our kids, your business, and your money. Margarita smiled and said, I've been telling the kids the news has it wrong and there's no way you're the Poetry Killer. I'll never let them think that I could believe you were capable of anything so clever.

But let me be clear with you, she said. You say anything to anybody, and I'll take the kids as far away as I can. We'll join Witness Protection and disappear from your life. They'll be as good as dead to you...

And that's how the worst day of my life became even worse. It's got to be unimaginable for my kids to be going through this. I don't even got the words. I don't believe Margarita would ever harm them, at least. If there ever was such a thing as love for her, it would be for her kids. But I have to prove my innocence to them and get out of here to be with them.

I had a hard time coming to terms with all of this and digesting Margarita as the Poetry Killer. I'm coming to terms with it, but my kids are in a lose-lose situation. They think I'm the Poetry Killer, which will scar them for life. If they find out Margarita is the Real Poetry Killer, they will still be scarred for life. What agony for them, either way. I would die a thousand deaths to shelter them from this pain. I need to talk to my grandma from the heavens, my guardian angel from the sky and ask for guidance and strength not just for myself but for my kids. I need to speak to a priest.

I guess that was a stupid question on my part. How could there have been a good, rational explanation for all the horrible things Margarita did? Sure, it could have been envy or greed, but what I saw in her eyes... Margarita is firkin nuts. She's telling herself some story in which she's the hero, but nobody else can figure out how that could be. I can hear her now, telling me, Don't dismiss me like that, and then she would retort with some kind of diagnosis.

I guess I should file for a divorce, but it's hard to think that I'll get a good deal when people think I'm a serial killer. How ironic, I was married to the Poetry Killer, and I'll probably die here in jail soon, anyways. She probably spent all my money and has taken over everything. Anyways, I'll never get my reputation back.

Chapter 18.

Dear Diary,

Egon came by to visit me in jail today and he said he believes me that I'm not the Poetry Killer. He went on to say he is treating the Fernanda case as open and he is still actively investigating it. I told Egon, I felt this coming but didn't want to believe it. Egon asked me, You felt what, Billy Bob? It's hard to explain, but I felt something bad was going to happen to me somehow, and that everything was to going to come crushing down on me. I knew Lt. Wienke suspected me, but I didn't think he would ever charge me because it would be impossible in my mind to charge someone who is not only innocent but has no real evidence against him. Egon tells me, Unfortunately, that's not the way the world works—it's not always fair, but stay patient! There will be a break in the case eventually. I don't believe you're the Poetry Killer, and I'm going to find out who did this to Fernanda and the rest of them.

I said, So you also believe it's only one person who is responsible for all the deaths at the Sun Brewing Motel? Egon said, I'm not entirely sure about that, but if you're accused of killing Fernanda and I find the real killer, then that would be grounds to set you free and exonerate you. I told him thanks for believing in me and that he was an unlikely ally. Egon replied, Perhaps, but it's what is right.

I said, I've been thinking about Fernanda. How do you think the body got all the way across the river, straight across from the motel? If you want to frame me at the motel, why move the body across the river? Egon responded, It is extremely odd. There were no footprints or tire marks, no sign of a boat being pulled ashore or pushed back out. Anyway, I'm going to go back to the crime scene today just to re-examine some things in the area. Sometimes walking around, not trying to focus too intensely on the details, you can find answers in plain sight. I responded, Good luck, because it seems to me there is only desolate desert out there.

As he was getting up to leave, I said, When was the last time you interviewed my wife, Margarita? Egon looked at me intensely and said, Why do you ask? The last time I talked to her, I said, she was acting strange. How so? Different, like I've never seen her act before.

Egon sat back down and looked hard at me. Billy Bob, are you trying to tell me you think your wife is involved in these murders in some way? I didn't know what else to say. Listen, Egon, I said, there are things I'm afraid to say because I'm afraid for my kids. I'm just asking when you last interviewed my wife. I know you'll be thorough in your investigation.

Egon rose slowly and nodded his head. I got it, Billy Bob. I'll be thorough, and I'll make sure no one has any reason to think you and I even had this conversation.

That was at least a glimmer of hope.

Just yesterday Lt. Wienke came by to taunt me and ask me what I wanted for my last supper. I said, You can't make up your mind if you want to kill me or make me rot in here. He said, I figure I'll explore my options, is all. Okay, then I'll have Granny's Southern fried chicken and Granny's Thanksgiving turkey and stuffing, mac and cheese because it was Analisa's favorite, Chico's Tacos also because it was Natasha's favorite, and chocolate chip cookies because that was Jesse James's favorite, with a glass of peach tea and absolutely no hot Cheetos! I can't talk to Wienke about

Margarita because I don't trust him. He would try to distort the truth and double down to hijack me somehow. I trust Egon and Chino.

I feel I'm regressing in jail. I don't know exactly how and in what ways, but I know I feel like I'm becoming some kind of animal in here—and it's not a lion, it's more like a honey badger. At first, I was in shock and kind of just staring at the walls with emptiness. I was going through a severe depression, feeling helpless, but now I'm in survival mode. Maybe that's actually a good thing.

Chapter 19.

Querido Diario,

Billy Bob always told me to keep writing and that writing helps me live twice, once in real life and the other in a better revision. I didn't know what he meant back then but now I get it. It's to bring a better perspective. That always helps me somehow, and writing in my diary helps me express myself in ways I wouldn't think of it previously in my life. I've become, in Billy Bob's words, very introspective, and I express myself when at times I thought that was next to impossible.

I went to see Billy Bob in jail again today and it was tough to see him that way. Billy Bob is not going to last long if he stays in a jail cell. There are different types of survival; Billy Bob can survive anything outside of being locked up. I think he will either commit suicide or provoke a violent altercation to live on the edge of death. He's not going to be able to adjust to being captured and contained for very long.

I survived prison and for a long time, but in many ways it's worse than dying. I've lived my life and I'm okay with it. I'm a lot older than Billy Bob. I'm becoming an old, old biker with a graying ZZ Top, Merlin-the-Wizard beard. I'm grateful that Billy Bob gave me a job, taught me brewing, and let me serve craft beer. I was never too hip, but I enjoyed watching all the hipsters coming and going and the zoo of The Sun Brewing Motel.

I know Billy Bob isn't The Poetry Killer. I need to help him as he helped me.

Maggie's funeral is tomorrow, and the rosary is tonight. Chino shows up for the rosary, and somewhat to his surprise, Margarita is there, too. As long as he'd been working at the motel, he'd never known Margarita to get very close to any of the staff; she always kept her distance. Egon is there, too, but Chino figures he may be watching for potential clues.

Margarita is clearly trying to blend in and not be noticed, which is difficult for a woman of her beauty to do. She's not social at all, this evening, or even attempting small talk to anyone. There are a lot of people and a lot of speakers. Chino got up there and spoke in the microphone to everyone. He gave a wonderful heart-felt speech for his co-worker, Maggie, whom he'd come to love and respect over the course of several years working together.

During the visitation afterward, Chino sees an opportunity to go talk to Margarita. He weaves through the crowd, circling around behind her so that she jumps when he appears at her side and says her name. Aye, Chino, you scared me! Oh, I'm sorry. I just saw you and wanted to say hi. This must all be ... I don't know, overwhelming for you. All these deaths at the motel. How are you holding up? She looked perturbed but answered, I'm holding up, thank you, Chino, but I have to go now. Chino stares stoically as she walks away. He knows she's up to no good.

Egon sat in the back row just observing everything. He noted who all attended, such as Peter and Chino and other staff, as well as Margarita, family, and friends. Egon studied every move Margarita made from her facial expressions to anything she said or did, including her posture. Egon watched as Chino said a few words to her. She appeared irritated and fidgety and walked away quickly. Suddenly, Egon was out of his seat and slipping through the crowd. He cut off Margarita near the front door. My condolences, madam. This has been a hard week for your family. She said, Yes, thank you, and continued to walk off. Egon said, Oh, ma'am, just one more thing. Could you use a napkin? A napkin? What on earth are you talking about? Forgive me, señora, I've noticed your fingers are stained with a red powder. Probably from eating hot Cheetos, right? I know you have a weak spot for them. She smiled and said, Yes, of course. Thank you. She grabbed the napkin, wiped her hands, and threw it on the ground. I've really got to get out of here. Good evening. Good evening, señora. He stepped aside and let her pass out the front door, then squatted down and picked up the napkin.

Often times when Chino was down and out, he would stay at the motel. Billy Bob would always make sure he had a place to stay. After Maggie's death, Chino takes a room at the motel again, but this time he also has ulterior motives. Something feels fishy, and he wants to keep his finger on the pulse of the Sun Brewing Motel while Billy Bob is locked up.

Chino is out the door to go to another day of work, though it's just not the same without Maggie and Billy Bob. There is no soul in the operation anymore. Margarita comes in to check on things, but she simply doesn't have the "it" factor with people. Whatever "it" is, she doesn't have it. People will do as she asks, but no one really respects her as a leader.

Chino's old rival, "El Diablo," shows up at the bar to drink some beers with his crew and take some rooms for the night. These bikers traveled from Tombstone, Arizona, from the annual Tombstone biker rally. They were all drinking, being loud, talking about how they had seen Jackyl live at the rally and that the lead singer was wearing the biggest cowboy hat they had ever seen while using a chainsaw. El Diablo is someone from Chino's past that he'd like to forget, but sometimes people's pasts won't stop bothering them. El Diablo used to make sexual advances to Chino's old lady back in the day and was always stabbing him in the back. And now he was annoying the customers at Chino's restaurant. Maybe it's karma. Chino is a firm believer in Karma. He always told Billy Bob, It comes back to you, carnalito. El Diablo and company are making noise, being rowdy and obnoxious, and generally pissing Chino off by their very presence.

El Diablo and his crew are celebrating a bit after the long haul of riding from Tombstone to Canutillo. Some of the bikers call it a day because it's been a long ride and settle in the motel rooms while El Diablo and a few others keep drinking on the patio overlooking the Rio Grande. El Diablo is the only one who has a room to himself, but he doesn't finally stumble into it until he is piss drunk and Chino turns off the patio lights. Chino watches the knucklehead limp down the walk to the rooms and sighs with relief. He managed to go the whole evening without being recognized and thus without getting into a fight with the worst human being in the world. He checks in with the night manager, Anna Maria, then goes back to his room to retire for the night.

The next morning, El Diablo's biker friends went to the front desk to check out. El Diablo isn't there, and he still isn't there after they have a late breakfast. Two of them go to check on him, but they come back and say he didn't answer when they knocked. They returned to the desk, where Peter has started his shift, and he went with them to knock on the door. No answer. Sir, your friends are worried about you, Peter called. If you don't answer, I'm going to open the door and come in. Still no response. Peter unlocked the door and opened it.

El Diablo is lying in his bed, dead, with an intramuscular syringe sticking out of his neck.

The police, along with Detective Pepe and the Ranger Wienke show up to secure the crime scene and investigate. Lt. Wienke discovers an empty vial with a scorpion stamp on it. John John Coffee is taking notes and recording the crime scene. Chino follows Wienke around demanding he release Billy Bob since the killer is clearly on the loose.

The reporters, including Iker Casillas and Elias Rockenstein from ABC news as well as some of the web sleuths who lived nearby all show up and start shouting questions from behind the police line. Is the Poetry Killer still on the loose? Did the killer use the same method as with the other victims? What information can you give us, detectives? The public has a right to know!

Margarita drives up to the motel and rushes inside to find Peter or Chino. Casillas and Rockenstein are on her as soon as they see her car. When she gets out, they put cameras in her face and start pelting her with questions. She seems overwhelmed and confused and even in shock. She says, This can't be happening. I just want all this to stop.

The sun rises on another day, and Chino goes into work for his shift. Margarita is already there, and there is an awkward tension between the two of them. Margarita looks curiously at Chino, and Chino smiles at her and asks how she is doing. Margarita smiles back, then walks away.

Chino has taken over management of the restaurant until Billy Bob gets back, but he spends the dinner hour behind the bar serving beer. A well-known regular sat at the bar with a friend and they began to discuss the latest incident a little more loudly than Chino would prefer. It has to be a copycat killer, he says, Because they already got Billy Bob, and he's the Poetry Killer. This guy was a local bearded-hipster type who wanted to be a professional brewer. He had ego and a little charisma and a lot of VC money behind him, but not much know-how, so he often came into the bar to try to gain business intelligence as if he was Billy Bob's close friend. Billy Bob would normally share with anyone who asked, but this guy had a way of trying to worm it out of a person rather than being direct and honest, and it rubbed everyone the wrong way. Billy Bob would always complain about these types of people. He'd say, I don't care what other people are doing, but they sure seem to care about everything that I do. I'm the most copied man alive, while they all go back to their little Instagram bubbles and claim to be innovative. It's one thing to do what others are doing, but it's an entirely different thing to knowingly and willingly cheat others and claim my ideas as their own, especially in magazines and television shows!

Chino bristles at this guy's callousness. He's a classic hater and frenemy. Finally, he can't help himself. He walks up to the guy and says, Are you seriously going to sit at Billy Bob's bar, after all he's done for you and how good he's been to you despite you stealing ideas from him left and right, and act like you know he's some kind of murdering monster? Hey, man, you just don't know with some people, you know? the guy says. I like Billy Bob as much as the next guy, but the police must have evidence if they arrested him. Billy Bob is innocent as a lamb, Chino says. Not about everything, maybe, but about these murders, for sure, and you'd do well not to talk poorly about a man while drinking his beer. Hey, I'm a paying customer, the guy says. I pays my money and I says what I like, and then I does what I like in my room all night.

You're staying here, tonight? Chino asks with some trepidation. That's right. It's already paid for and everything. Planning to live it up tonight? Some, but not too much. I'm meeting a girl here later. I need to stay lucid enough to perform, if you know what I mean. Yeah, everyone always knows what you mean. I thought you were married? says Chino, pointing at the guy's wedding ring. The hipster shrugs. That doesn't bother some girls. Anyway, this place has, like, a mystical vibe, you know? What happens here, it's like it's happening in a different reality. Oh yeah, how do you think your wife would feel about that? My wife's probably high as a kite right now and none the wiser. Anyway, I got this idea that I'm going to sleep with every woman that works in my brewery. Then maybe I'll settle down and do the straight thing.

Chino goes around back to the kitchen where he runs into Margarita. She's fuming. Oh, did you hear that? he asks her. I ought to put a gag ball in his mouth to shut him up then dump his beer on his face, she says. I've never heard you talk that way, Margarita, but I could get used to it. That guy's just the worst; I wish he'd stop coming by here. Well, she says, maybe we can do something to persuade him that this isn't a good place for him to come around. Hey, if you've got an idea, let me know how I can help.

Meanwhile, Egon goes back to the crime scene where Fernanda was found, not really expecting to find anything but to walk around just before sunset and let his brain play with the problem. Mexican cowboys ride by on roan, pale, and palomino horses; in Mexico, a lot of people still use horses as transportation. The Mexican cowboys stop for a moment to drink some water out of their bota bags, and the horses make some noise with their hooves. They wave at Egon and he waves back. As the cowboys leave, Egon walks over to where the horses were standing. He thought he heard a funny sound when the horses beat the ground. It sounded more like a hard object, similar to wood, than to the dull earth. Egon gets down on the ground and starts brushing the dirt around. He uncovers a small wooden door, maybe 3' x 3'. He lifts the door and sees a shaft going down into the ground.

Egon goes back to his vehicle, calls for back up, and gets a flashlight. Then he goes down the metal ladder into what appears to be a tunnel. A smuggling tunnel for the coyotes, is his first thought. It's a deep shaft going straight down, with reinforced metal and wood logs framing out the tunnel. While he's still standing beneath the door, he radios back to his base to let them know what he is doing, but he expects to lose his signal when he walks a few steps down the tunnel. Not far down, he finds an old wooden cabinet. It's dusty but also shows signs of recent use. He opens the top drawer and finds a hot Cheetos bag inside. He checks all the drawers until he finally gets to the bottom drawer and finds a 5 ml vial with a scorpion stamped on it, in a plastic bag with a few 22-gauge intramuscular needles. Egon leaves everything in the cabinet and continues to cautiously move forward. He thought he was heading north, but now he's not so sure. The river would have to be deeper than the tunnel, he figures.

Then he hears something. He shuts off his flashlight and waits. Then he sees a light coming his way from the opposite end of the tunnel. He slowly and quietly moves his hand to his pistol, unlatches the holster, draws it, and pulls back the hammer. Whoever it is gets closer and closer. They are pushing or pulling something that rattles and squeaks. Egon lifts his gun and walks towards the silhouette that appears before him. He points his gun at center mass and shouts, Don't move or I'll shoot!

It's Chino! Egon sees Chino with a big, 4-wheeled wheelbarrow that he is toting a bearded hipster-looking man in. Egon said, Don't move, Chino, and keep your hands where I can see them. Alright, now slowly raise your hands above your head. Make one wrong move and you're dead. I'll kill you Chino.

Chapter 20.

Dear Diary,

I never thought I would get caught. I just wanted to do enough to cause doubt for Billy Bob's case to be thrown out so that he can be set free as a bird. I thought planting that Cheetos wrapper would point them in the right direction, but that didn't matter when Egon caught me in the tunnel with that pain in the ass hipster brewer. I'm in the slammer again but this time for the rest of my life, which won't be much considering my age. I confessed to being The Poetry Killer. At least my friend Billy Bob will get set free again but I don't envy him for what he is going to have to deal with, getting his life back together and dealing with that psychopath wife of his.

We know Margarita is the real Poetry Killer, but I chose El Diablo as an old score that needed to be settled. El Diablo was unfinished business. When you're from the rough and dangerous neighborhoods that I come from and have my background then you will wait many years to get even with someone. The bearded hipster simply got on my nerves for the last time, we're just cut from a different cloth. He's a slimy rodent but served a purpose. The world is better off without him anyways.

I notice things, especially because I'm not in the kitchen slaving away on a hot grill for hours like Billy Bob. I've lived in The Sun Brewing Motel and have been working there for a very long time, since the beginning. I figured out long ago about the secret passageways in *The Sun Brewing Motel*. The first clue was the cuckoo clocks mounted to the walls in a certain position in all the rooms. The cuckoo clocks were there to be able to see the most area, as if someone was trying to see the best angle for watching what's going on in the rooms. What really tipped me off was when Billy Bob showed me his secret door behind the bookshelf many years ago. I knew there had to be more and I was right. There is a secret passageway that runs behind every room in the motel and in that passageway there is a small sliding metal cover over the peep holes that goes into the cuckoo clocks. You move the sliding metal cover and you can see a good portion in the room and you move it back when you're finished. The cuckoo clocks are so elaborate in design and big enough to conceal it. Billy Bob doesn't know that I know about these secret passageways. I checked it out myself and I found a hidden door in the floor that goes to an underground tunnel going underneath the Rio Grande and into Mexico. I've known about this hidden tunnel for a long time. When these murders started happening, I checked the tunnel out, doing my own little investigations. I found evidence of vials, needles, and hot Cheetos. I suspected it was Margarita all along and was waiting for her to get caught, but she never did, and instead Billy Bob got blamed which wasn't right.

I tried to make El Diablo and the bearded hipster's murders look like they were from The Poetry Killer.

I guess I did a good enough job. I knew the murders were an inside job and frankly at first I suspected Margarita, but then I knew it was Margarita without anyone even telling me. But how do you tell your best bud that his wife may be a murderous psychopath? And so here we are.

It's been all over the news for weeks: The real Poetry Killer has been caught, and Billy Bob has been exonerated. Iker Casillas and Elias Rockenstein are there for ABC KVIA news filming Billy Bob as he is released. Casillas asks Billy Bob, How does it feel to be exonerated? ...How does it feel to get your freedom back and to see your family again? Billy Bob has an empty look on his face, and with a stoic demeanor replies, It's good to be free. Now I need to try to get my life back on track. I've done some soul searching and praying. I found Jesus in jail, and I need to be born again.

Some time later, Billy Bob and Egon are walking in the desert up the famous Mount Cristo Rey. At the top of Mount Cristo Rey is a large monument statue of Jesus on the Cross, and on the other side of the mountain is Mexico. Egon tells Billy Bob, It's poetic justice, in a way. I've always been interested in justice more than the intricate workings of the system. Billy Bob replies, I know what you mean. Lt. Wienke is a rules, systems, and institutions guy rather than a justice guy. It's poetic justice because Chino got caught committing murder, so he deserves to spend the rest of his life in prison, and you got set free because you're not the Poetry Killer. But we both know Chino isn't the Poetry Killer, either.

Billy Bob says, I know that, but how do you know that? Chino was sloppy. The last two victims were personal to him, while all the other ones are a stretch at best for motive. I believe he did it to give the appearance that the Poetry Killer is still on the loose and therefore not you. Billy Bob replied, but if you know it's not him, can you bring in the real killer?

It doesn't work that way, amigo. I have no jurisdiction in Texas. I can tell the ranger what I think, but it's up to him to act on the evidence. Unfortunately, I don't have enough evidence to convict Margarita.

So, you know it's her, then, says Billy Bob. Yeah, I figured, says Egon. Her family owned the place before you, so if anyone knew about the secret tunnels it would be her. She's got the medical training to understand toxins and the deep connections to Mexico to find an underground source. She was a decathlete in college, I'm sure you know, so she could shoot a gun, or even a dart gun. And the people that went missing all either flirted with you, got too close to you, or insulted you in some way, so it had to be someone whose identity was wrapped up in you. Thing is, Chino matches a lot of that, too. I just don't think he's smart enough to carry it all off. Specially the way those passages were swept clean so we knew someone had been there but couldn't find any prints. No, she's got us over a barrel on this one. The best thing for Chino is to tell the truth, try to only get charged on the two murders and not the whole shebang.

Billy Bob and Egon are at the top of Mount Cristo Rey after a long walk up the mountain. The wind is blowing hard at that high altitude and they can see all of the borderlands from way up in the sky. They also see all the candles that were lit and crosses with pictures of loved ones by the colossal monument cross. I should go thank him for setting me free, Billy Bob said. But he shouldn't have murdered those people, I don't care how much he cared for me. Egon responds, Chino is an old gang member from back in the day. He was a misguided youth who found a guide as an adult—but then his guide got locked up. He was coming up when gangs were running rampant in the borderlands. Chino sees El Diablo as a casualty of war. It doesn't make it right, but that's how someone like Chino operates.

Billy Bob says, He's my best friend and it makes me sad it's ending this way for him. Chino has a lot of good qualities and is a good person.

I guess that's the duality of man.

Life can be strange, Egon. Margarita is at home all smiles with the kids, and Chino is the most loyal soldier I've ever known and now he is in prison. Egon replies, Chino murdered two people and got what is just. Well, if I know Chino, he is going to make jailhouse hooch and prison wine out of his toilet; he is incredibly resourceful.

You know, Egon, Billy Bob continued, I've had a lot of time to think about things, especially in jail. You're right that Margarita was wrapped up in me. Toward the end, there, it was like she was taking on my personality as her own. It was strange: Margarita talked to Maggie before she died, and Maggie said it was odd that Margarita was talking like I sometimes do. She asked, How close are you to your grandma? and then she said, Grandma always said, if you can't say something nice then don't say anything at all.

That's something I would always say. I used to say that to the kids all the time. If I ever asked anyone how close they were to their grandma, it was because I wanted to talk about how close I was to mine and what I learned from her. It's like Margarita was twisting my own saying for her own evil ways.

Everything I would take an interest in, she would take an interest in, but it was as if she was becoming me somehow. It's hard to explain, but I've seen it. It was her idea to dedicate them beers to Maggie and for the names. It was Margarita who wanted the beer Fernanda made. It was Margarita who wanted the beer Rio de Piedad made from filtered river water. I was always big on indigenous beers using ingredients from our region. Everything I've mentioned that I wanted to do, Margarita wanted it also in all the beers that were for the victims. I just wanted to make her happy.

All those times I came home from work dead tired from working 12 to 20 hours a day then fell asleep... You know, sometimes I woke up feeling like I had been drugged or something, but of course I had no reason to suspect anything. I felt that way every time I woke up to another victim. Prime example was when I woke up to the news Maggie had been murdered. I felt foggy and confused and wasn't sure even where I was.

And I didn't know about the underground tunnel, but I think I knew most of them secret passageways. I left them alone and abandoned them; they were never in use, so someone could easily have been prowling around in there without anyone knowing.

So now it's all coming together, but I still would have never dreamed that Margarita was the Poetry Killer if she hadn't told me herself. Even then, I was so shocked from being arrested that I wasn't sure I heard her right. That's a strange position to be in, and it took a while for it to sink in. I'm still at a loss on what to do exactly, but I know that I want my kids away from her and I want this nightmare to end.

Egon, imagine how the kids would react to being taken away from their mother? All they know for all their lives is how she nurtures, cares for them, and is their best friend. Life simply isn't fair sometimes. This just goes against the firkin rules of the universe.

Egon replies, This walk up the mountain has helped you Billy Bob. I can see it already. Here we are at the top of the mountain looking at one of the most beautiful monuments in the entire world and viewing the entire borderlands with the wind at our backs. I asked you once if you were a religious man, do you remember? Billy Bob says, Yep, I do.

Egon says, Being way up here looking over the borderlands is spiritual.

Have faith and hope.

Breathe the fresh air and be grateful for today.

Billy Bob's phone buzzes and the song "Wooden Jesus" by Temple of the Dog starts playing. Billy Bob stops and stares at Egon. It's Margarita calling.

The End.

The Brewers' Murder Diaries - Vol I.